Alfred Tennyson

IN
MEMORIAM

悼念集

汉英双语

[英]丁尼生 著
张定浩 译
翁海贞 校

上海文艺出版社

目录

1　悼念集

223　In Memoriam

445　译后记

463　附录：永生颂

悼念集

序 曲 *

刚强的上帝之子,不朽的爱,
 我们这些未曾目睹你容颜的人
 信奉你,因着信,仅凭着信,
在无力证实处也相信。

你拥有这些闪光和幽暗的星球;
 你创造人与兽的生命;
 你创造死亡;瞧,你的足
踏在你所创造的头骨之上。

你不会把我们遗弃于尘土:
 你创造了人类,他不知其缘由,
 他认为自己并非生来有死;
而你已然将这样的他创造:你是正义。

你似人,又似神,
 最高的,最神圣的人子,是你。
 我们的意志,是迷惘不安的意志;
我们的意志,是履行你的意志。

* 这首诗,虽然作为序曲,但如同大多数序言一般,其实是写于整本诗集完成之后。本书所有注释均为译者注。

人类微弱的文明自有时日，
　　它们风光一时，又沉寂消亡：
　　它们只是你破碎的光，
而远远大于它们的，主啊，是你。

我们唯余信：我们是无知的人；
　　因为知识关乎我们眼所能见的事物，
　　但我们相信那最终的知识来自于你，
一道黑暗中的光：让它生长。

让知识日益增长，但与此相伴的
　　是我们内心不断增长的敬畏；
　　心智和灵魂，配合完美，
可以合奏出宛如从前又更为宽广的

音乐。我们是愚蠢和虚妄；
　　当我们不知畏惧之际我们嘲弄你：
　　但请帮助你愚蠢的子民去承受；
帮助你众多自负的尘世去承受你的光。

请原谅我貌似无法根除的罪；
　　原谅我这一生貌似获得的成就；

因为这些功过只在人类中间游走，
而无法波及你的面前，我的主。

请原谅我为一位逝者而生出的悲恸，
　　他是你的造物，如此美丽。
　　他相信他活在你的内部，那是
我察觉他更值得被爱的地方。

请原谅这些狂乱的恍惚的哭泣，
　　一位虚掷年华的青年的困境；
　　原谅那些错失真理的日子
请让我得以明智，在你的智慧中。

1849 年

纪念哈勒姆

逝于 1833 年

一

我曾相信,正如面对一架明净竖琴　　*指歌德。
　　演绎出千种音调的他*所相信的,
　　人类会以他们死去的自身
作为阶石,迈向更高的事物。

然而有谁会把岁月这般预示,
　　定要在失去中寻回相称的收获?
　　或是再伸出一只手,穿越时间去拾掇
那些泪水在久远之后的利息?

让爱紧抓住痛苦以免一起沉溺,
　　让黑暗保持她渡鸦的光泽。
　　哦,因为与丧失对酌,
与死亡共舞,且顿足踏地,

这些都要好过时间这个得胜者的姿态,
　　它只会嘲笑爱的徒劳,并夸耀说,
　　"瞧那个人,爱过,失去过,
但他所有的存在,也只剩下形骸。"

二

老紫杉，你设法抓紧那些石碑，
　　它们讲述躺在下面的死者的名字，
　　你的细枝网住没有梦的头颅，
你的根茎缠绕在那些骨头周围。

季节催动花朵再次开放，
　　且催动头生的鸟畜簇拥成群；
　　而在由你所构成的幽暗里，钟声
敲打出人们细小的生命。

你不关心绚烂与盛开，
　　也不会在任何的大风中改变，
　　烙铁的夏日也丝毫不能
触动你年深日久的荫郁：

凝望着你，忧郁之树，
　　渴慕你无比顽固的坚毅，
　　我好像也渐渐失去血气，
渐渐融入了你的身躯。

三

哦忧伤,这残忍的伴侣,

　　死之墓穴中的女祭司,

　　甜美与苦痛在呼吸间交替,

你撒谎的唇在低语些什么?

"群星,"她低语道,"盲目运转;

　　一张网在天宇铺开;

　　一声呼喊自荒芜处传来,

垂死的太阳在呢喃:

"所有的幽灵,罪人*,起立,

　　(伴随全部以她为名的乐章,

　　以及我自身的一个空洞回音)

双手空垂于空洞的形体。"

* Nature,在这里大写,在基督教语境中有时指"未受天恩的罪人状态",故酌情翻译成"罪人"。

然而我会如此盲目地接受

　　且将她视为一种善性来拥抱吗?

　　还是说,一旦她踏上心智的门槛,

就像碾碎一种罪孽那样碾碎她?

四

我睡着了,卸掉一切防备;
　　愿意志臣服于黑暗;
　　我蜷缩进无舵的小船,
自言自语,任思绪纷飞:

我的心,你现在处于何种境地,
　　你的欲望已丧失殆尽,
　　也几乎不敢再询问,
"那令我艰于跳动的,是什么?

是一些你已然失去之物,
　　一些过往岁月的欢乐。
　　碎吧,你这深瓶,里面盛放的
寒冷泪水,哀痛将之晃动成冰!

这些不可名状的阴云横亘
　　于那昏暗眼睑下的长夜
　　直到意志随着清晨醒转,并呼喊,
"你不可就这么愚蠢地沉沦。"

五

将自我感受的哀痛付诸文字,
　我有时以为这仿佛是一种罪愆,
　因为言语,犹如自然,半是呈现
半是将那内在的灵魂藏匿。

然而,对于永不安宁的头脑与心灵,
　字斟句酌的语言自有价值;
　那不足为道的技艺练习,
令痛苦麻木,似慢性毒品。

诗句,犹如黑纱,我用它裹住自己,
　犹如用粗陋麻衣抵御寒冷;
　但那在词语包裹下的巨大哀痛
仍显出它的轮廓,且就如此而已。

六

有人写道,"依旧有别的朋友",
 "失去是人生之常态"——
 而常态就是没有什么可奇怪,
是空谷壳脱离谷粒的理由。

失去是一种常态,这说法不会
 减轻我失去时的苦涩,反倒加重:
 太平常!就像清晨的光从来无法走进
黑夜,但有一些心已破碎。

做父亲的,无论身在何处,
 正举杯向你远方英勇的儿子致意;
 杯酒未干,枪声响起,
那来自你的生命律动已然停驻。

做母亲的,祈祷上帝会救取
 你的水手,——当你垂首默想,
 他那挂上铅球的帆布尸床
正坠入浩瀚浑茫的坟墓。

你们毫不知情,正如我

  在他临终时刻还写信将他问候;

  还凝思于我想倾诉的一切,

有些已写下,有些尚在揣摩;

依然期待他出现在家园;

  期待在他习惯的路上与他相遇;

  怀抱祝愿,想着,"就在今日,"

抑或,"他会来的,在明天。"

某处,温顺如鸽的懵懂女孩,

  坐着将金发细细梳理;

  并欣悦于自己的美丽,

可怜的孩子,在等待你的爱!

此刻她父亲的壁炉烟囱闪亮

  期待一位客人的到来;

  她拿起一枝玫瑰或是一根缎带,

并想着,"这将最使他欣赏";

因为他将在今晚见到它们;

  她想象那情景,脸颊绯红;

已经离开妆台的她,又转身对镜
再次理好一缕长长的鬈发;

就在她转身的刹那,那噩运
　　已注定,她未来的夫君
　　已溺毙于他所穿越的浅滩,
抑或从马上坠落而亡。

哦,对她而言结局将会怎样?
　　对我而言还能剩下什么美好之物?
　　在她,是成为永恒的少女,
在我,是不会再有另外的朋友。

七

漆黑的房子,我再次驻足停留
   在这有点乏味的无尽长街上,
   那个我心曾激烈跳动的地方,
那扇门,在等待一只手,

一只再也不能握住的手——
   看着我,因我的长夜难眠,
   像一个有罪者般步履悄然
潜向那扇门,在晨曦初开的时候。

他不在这儿;然而在远处
   生活的噪音重新升起,
   空虚的曙光鬼魅一般穿过
这寥落长街上的细雨。

八

一位幸福的爱者前来看望
　　深爱自己的情人,
　　他燃烧着,按响门铃,
却得知她已不在,远离家乡;

他黯然神伤,所有梦幻的灯
　　顷刻熄灭,从门厅至卧室
　　到处一片漆黑,所有的
房间都死气沉沉:

与之相似,我发现
　　那些我们时常相聚过的美好地方,
　　郊外,屋内,大街上,
都因你的不在而陷入黑暗。

而那位在昔日踪迹处
　　徘徊游荡的爱者,或许会发现
　　一朵小花正随风雨轻颤,
那是她曾细心照料过的花束;

同样,对于你——我那被遗弃的心,
　　在我深深的憾意中也是如此,
　　还有我这点诗才所生出的小花,
纵无暇照料,也不曾褪色。

但既然它曾愉悦过业已消失的眼目,
　　我就要在他的坟前把它栽下,
　　倘若它能活着,让它在那里开花,
抑或枯萎,至少可以在那里死去。

九

明媚之船,从意大利的港口启程
  驶过温和宁静的海的平原,
  载着我所失去的亚瑟被爱着的遗骸,
请扬起你的翅膀,送他回来。

把他带给家里那些徒然
  哀悼的人;轻快的航速
  弄皱了你桅杆的倒影,带着
他的灵柩,穿过滚滚浪涛。

愿整个夜晚没有狂风侵扰
  你的滑动龙骨,直到晨星,明亮
  如我们纯粹的爱,穿过晨曦
在带露的甲板上铺洒它的微光。

愿四方的星光能点亮航程;
  睡吧,温柔的天空,在船首入睡[*];
  睡吧,温柔的海风,就像如今的他那样安睡,
我的朋友,我挚爱的兄弟;

[*] 表示没有逆风。

我的亚瑟,我再也无法见到他,
  直至我鳏居生涯的尽头;
  我爱他超出了手足的情谊,
就像一个儿子爱着他的母亲。

十

我听见船底龙骨扬波;
　　我听见钟声敲开夜晚:
　　我看见舷窗闪闪;
我看见水手在掌舵。

你把水手还给他的妻子,
　　从异乡领回浪游者;
　　把信笺交于颤抖的双手;
你还承载黑色的重负,一具消散的生命。

我们心想,就将他这么带回吧,
　　这平静的面容就是如此满足
　　我们落叶归根的幻想。对于
我们这些凡人,似乎比较完美的

就是在三叶草的土地下面安息,
　　汲取阳光和雨水,
　　或是在那圣坛之上,村庄跪着
慢慢饮干圣杯中的酒;*

* 此段喻指两种墓地,教堂院子里的墓地和室内尸骨存放所,末句意谓村民在老圣安德烈教堂做礼拜。

而不是和你在一起,那汹涌的旋涡

  会将他吞入有咸味的渊薮。

  而他的曾时常与我相扣的手,

会随着海藻和贝壳颠簸。*

* 此段暗指向《约拿书》2:5:"诸水环绕我,几乎淹没我;深渊围住我,海草缠绕我的头。"

十一

平静是清晨没有一丝声响,
  平静得像要顺应更为平静的悲哀,
  唯有那穿过颓败枝叶的
栗子,正啪嗒落在地上:

平静和深沉的安宁在这高地荒野,
  在这些将金雀花浸透的露水之上,
  在所有银白蛛丝之上
闪烁成青绿与金黄的明灭:

平静和寂寂的光在那边的旷原,
  它随着秋日的林荫到处延展,
  经过拥挤的庄园和渐渐疏落的教堂尖塔,
与奔腾的海洋融成一片:

平静和深沉的安宁在这长空下,
  这些叶子染红直至坠落;
  而在我的心里,就算是平静,
哪怕一丝,也是绝望的平静:

平静在那海上，在银色的长眠里，
　　波浪轻摇着波浪进入休憩，
　　在那宏伟的胸膛里有死一般的平静
它起伏，只随着深深的海在起伏。

十二

瞧，就像一只鸽子腾空而起，
　　承受着悲哀的故事穿越天宇，
　　一些忧伤的讯息会织入
她急切振动的羽翼；

我难以停留；也像她这般飞去；
　　剩下这凡人的方舟，
　　剩下这失神的形骸，在身后，
我离开这海边峭壁，匆促

越过宽广如球镜的海面，
　　抵达南方天空的热浪，
　　看船帆浮现在远方，
徘徊哭泣在它边缘，

继而说道："就这样来临，我的友人？
　　这就是我心心念念的一切的结局？"
　　继而盘旋，在空中呜咽：
"这就是结局？这就是结局？"

我再度向前飞掠,游曳
　　在船首四周,再转身
　　返回躯体坐思之处,
得知我已恍惚了半个时辰。

十三

那鳏夫的眼泪就这般滑落,
    当他梦见新亡人的模样,
    并移动他狐疑的手臂,
察觉她的位置空冷无着;

这眼泪哀悼一种始终在场的丧失,
    哀悼在心心相印处的空洞;
    而在那温暖的手曾相依相握之处,
只剩下沉默,直到我也沉默。

这眼泪哀悼我选中的伴侣,
    一个可怕的想法,一个生命的消失,
    我爱的充满仁慈的人,
成为一个灵,不再有呼吸和声音。

来吧时间,慢慢地教我,
    让我不会在梦中痛苦;
    但如今这些事情尚显得如此突兀,
我的眼泪依旧忍不住地掉落;

我想象能有足够的时间振翅而起,
  环视即将到来的船帆,
  仿佛他们带来的唯有商人的特产,
而不曾带来什么沉重的躯体。

十四

倘若有一人前来报信于我,
　　说你今日已抵达这片陆地,
　　我就会即刻奔下码头,
就会见到你在港口停泊;

然后伫立,紧裹着悲哀,
　　会见到你的乘客们正依次
　　向他们的亲友摇手示意,
并轻快地踏过跳板而来;

而倘若那个我称为半神的男人
　　也随这些人而来;
　　也抓住我的手热烈摇摆,
把各种家长里短一一询问;

我就会告诉他我全部的伤痛,
　　以及生活近来是如何失落,
　　而他会为我感到难过,
并诧异于我脑海中的胡思乱想;

然后我会察觉不到一丝变化,
　　他整个形体毫无死亡的迹象,
　　我只会发现他依然完好无损,
我不会觉得这一切的发生有什么奇怪。

十五

今夜狂风骤起,
　　自落日之地咆哮:
　　将最后的红叶卷离树梢,
将白嘴鸦吹散天际;

森林噼啪作响,大水翻腾,
　　牛群在草地上聚成一团;
　　冲破塔楼和树林而来的日光,
又横扫过整个尘世:

倘若不是幻象,在坚称
　　你正完整而轻柔地横越
　　一片平静如镜的海面,
我几乎不能承受

这呼啸于枯枝上的紧张与骚动,
　　倘若不是担心船只的命运,
　　我因悲哀而生的狂乱之心
也许会着迷和专注于那远处的流云,

它向上攀升,愈来愈高,
　　拖着一种疲乏的心绪向前,
　　又倾覆于沉闷的西天,
一座火光中隐现的棱堡。

十六

这些从我飘落的言辞究竟为何?
　　平静的绝望和狂野的不安是否可以
　　在同一个胸膛中共处,
或许悲伤就是这么变幻莫测?

或许这悲伤只不过在表面
　　变换着平静与风暴,
　　但这悲伤的深处并不理解
事物的流变?犹如那些死寂深潭

只能在表面映照出一小方蓝天
　　以及掠过蓝天的云雀的影子。
　　或许我是被这突如其来的打击
所迷惑,如不幸的船板

在夜里撞向一块崎岖暗礁,
　　在沉没之前盲目摇晃?
　　这打击摧毁我思考的力量
以及所有关于自我的认知;

使我成为那个发狂的男人
　　他的幻觉熔合了新旧,
　　让真假一同闪现,
再毫无计划地把一切拖入混沌?

十七

你来了，我哭泣已久：这微风
　　推动你的船帆，而我的祷词
　　也像这细细游动的气息，
吹拂着你越过孤寂的海洋。

因为我在心里看见你穿越
　　这一圈圈海平线的束缚，
　　周而复始，日落日出，
快来，你带来我爱的一切。

此后，无论你在哪儿远航，
　　我的祝福都如一道光，
　　日夜投射于广漠的海面，
如一座守护你还乡的灯塔。

无论暴风雨怎样在海中肆虐，
　　愿它赦免你，神圣的小船；
　　愿温馨的露珠悄然
自群星深处滴落，在夏夜。

这项仁慈的使命已实现,
　　你带来如此珍贵的遗骨;
　　在我鳏居人生的终点处,
尘归尘,我将再次与他相见。

十八

好了,就这样吧,我们会立在
　　这片安葬他的英国大地,
　　从他的尘灰中会长出
故乡的紫罗兰。

这念头微弱,但它似已成真,
　　犹如平静的骨骸已得到赐福,
　　休憩在家族成员的碑牌间,
休憩在度过青春的地方。

那么来吧,纯洁的手,托住熟睡的
　　或是佩戴好睡眠面具的,头颅,
　　来吧,所有爱哭泣的,
来聆听死者的葬礼。

然而,然而,倘若可能,
　　与他心心相印的我,
　　愿意把呼吸注入他的唇,
把我奄奄一息的生命分给他;

那生命没有死去，只是忍受痛苦，
　　缓慢形成更坚定的心智，
　　珍藏那再也看不见的面容，
那再也听不见的言辞。

十九

<small>* 哈勒姆 1833 年 9 月死于多瑙河水流过的维也纳，他 1834 年 1 月被埋葬于英国瓦伊河畔的克利夫登教堂，瓦伊河又与英国最长的河流塞汶河相连，所以说是多瑙河交还给塞汶河。塞汶河在大西洋布里斯托海峡入海，和中国的钱塘江一样也会有潮汐倒灌的现象。</small>

多瑙河交还给塞汶河 *
　那不再跳动的黯淡的心；
　他们把他埋在美好的岸边，
那儿能听见流水的声音。

那儿塞汶河一天涨潮两次；
　咸涩的海水流过，
　令半条潺潺的瓦伊河沉默，
让山地蒙上一丝静谧。

被迫沉默的瓦伊河不再流淌，
　同时被迫沉默的还有我最深的痛苦，
　当泪珠盈眶却不能流出，
销愁的歌便在我心中鼓荡。

潮汐回落，流水的声音再度
　在两岸林木间响起；
　我更深的哀痛也平息，
这时我才能略微将这些讲述。

二十

那些次要的、可以言说的悲痛,
  低语着千种脆弱的誓言,
  犹如那些家里面
刚刚遭遇主人亡故的仆人;

他们倾诉如此这般的情感,
  这悲痛完全一目了然:
  "太难了,"他们说,"去发现
另一个像这样值得侍奉的人家。"

我较为肤浅的情绪也与之类似,
  可以在言辞中渐渐获得安顿;
  但仍有其他内在的悲痛,
而眼泪尚未涌出就已冻结;

因为那些孩子即便坐在炉火边,
  也被死亡的寒意所侵袭,
  难以呼吸,他们即便走来走去
也如同无声无息的幻影:

但没有任何公开的交谈,
　　这些有活力的小精灵如此沮丧地
　　望着空椅子,一边想着
"多么和蔼!多么可亲!然而他已不见。"

二十一

我向躺卧在地下的他唱歌,
  而既然青草在我四周摇曳,
  我就摘取一些墓上的草叶,
把它们当作可以吹响的口哨。

过路人偶尔听到我的歌声,
  有时其中一个人会严厉地说:
  "这个人会让软弱的更软弱,
会融化掉人们蜡制的心。"

另一个人回答,"随他去,
  他就爱炫耀痛苦,
  凭借哨声他或许会赢取
所谓忠贞不渝的赞美。"

第三个人则大为恼怒:"这难道是
  吟唱个人空洞悲歌的时候吗?
  当越来越多的人们蜂拥追逐
公民权利的席位与王座,

"这难道是颠倒与痴迷的时候么?

  当科学向前伸展她的手臂

  探索一个又一个世界,哄诱

最新发现的星辰也交出秘密。"

瞧,你们说的都是徒劳:

  你们根本不认识那神圣的骸骨:

  我歌唱只因为我必须如此,

我的哨声不过就像红雀的啁啾:

一只喜悦;音调欢快,

  因她如今已儿女成行;

  另一只悲伤;音调走样,

因她的雏鸟被偷偷夺走。

二十二

树林里有一条我们并肩走过的路,
　　曾洒满我们的欢乐,
　　起起伏伏,穿过四载甜美的光阴,
一次次的春去秋来,花开雪落:

我们一路轻歌笑语,
　　享受季节带给我们的一切,
　　四月去了又来,
我们长久置身于五月的欢愉:

然而那条我们并肩走过的路
　　在第五个秋季悄然下陡*,
　　当我们随希望之神向下走,
尽头端坐着人所畏惧的阴影;

他拆散了我们美好的友情,
　　张开他黑暗冰冷的斗篷,
　　把你在其中裹作一团,
且闷住你低语的唇,

*指1833年9月哈勒姆突然病逝。

带你去往我无法看见也无法
　　跟随之地,尽管我步履匆促,
　　边走边想,在荒原某处,
那阴影也坐在那等我。

二十三

现在,我的悲哀有时也会喑哑,
  抑或只会断断续续地歌唱,
  独自,独自,去往他曾待过的地方,
那黑影从头至脚遮着斗篷,

他保有所有教义的秘钥,
  我徘徊,时而趔趄,
  回顾我的来处,
或向着这道路的尽头;

然后哭泣,有怎样的变化已发生,
  道路两侧的树叶都在说话;
  而所有丰盛的丘陵将哼出
一个快乐的潘的低语。

我俩轮流做彼此的向导,
  幻想自幻想汲取灵感;
  在与言语结合之前,
思想已急切地与思想结合;

我们所遇皆是善好,
　　时间所带来的一切皆是善好,
　　所有春天的秘密
流动成血液里的生机;

许多古老的哲学
　　在希腊人的高地上庄严歌唱,
　　所有环绕我们的灌木林
回荡着阿卡迪亚的长笛。

二十四

我曾有的欢乐时日难道
  真是纯粹完美如我所言?
  那白日光艳灼灼的源泉
也定然掺杂黑夜的浮岛。*

         * 这两行喻指太
          阳和太阳黑子。

如果我们所遇皆是善好,
  这个尘世已成为天堂
  但人类从未见过天堂,
自从太阳第一次升起又下沉。

是无边的悲痛
  让从前的欢乐显得如此强烈?
  是眼前的失落
才将过去一一凸显?

或者,过去总是会赢得
  荣耀,因它存在于远处;
  它自行运转成我们看不见的
完美星辰,当我们在其中转动?

二十五

我知道这就是生活——
　　生活就是我们曾共同面对的道路；
　　当时，和现在一样，
生活为我们的脊背准备每日的重负。

但正是这重负迫使我的步履
　　如空中承载信笺的青鸟一般轻盈；
　　我爱我不得不承受的重量，
因它欲求着爱的帮助：

我不会有任何身心的疲倦，
　　既然强力的爱会将这满舱的疼痛
　　劈成相等的两份，
其中一半，交给他帮我分担。

二十六

沉闷干燥的路仍向前蜿蜒着；
　我随它一起；因为我渴望证实
　爱不会被时间的流逝所侵蚀，
无论善变的舌头如何言说。

而如果那观看罪与善的
　眼睛，确有能力看出
　那在绿色内部朽坏的树，
以及一建造就坍塌的塔楼——

哦，如果那双眼真可以预见
　或看出（在祂里面没有从前）
　更长久的生命未必就更真实，
而爱也会变得漠然，

那么，在晨曦划开印度洋的海波
　抵达这里之前，我就可以找到
　死神，他正怀揣密钥
等待覆盖我，令我从自嘲中解脱。

二十七

我一点都不会妒忌
　　这缺乏高贵愤怒的囚徒,
　　这出生于笼中的红雀,
从未见识过夏日的林地:

我不妒忌那野兽
　　它在无尽的时间里尽情放纵,
　　不受负罪感的约束,
从未有可供唤醒的良知;

也不妒忌那所谓的幸福,
　　那从未缔结过誓约的心
　　只会在怠惰的野草中沉滞,
我不妒忌任何冷漠生出的安宁。

我坚持这一点,无论发生什么;
　　越是悲痛,我对此感受越深;
　　宁可爱过又失去
也不愿从未爱过。

二十八 *

时间逼近基督的诞辰:
  月隐没;夜晚寂静;
  山丘间起伏的圣诞钟声 †
薄雾中彼此应答。

周围四村庄的四套钟声,
  由远及近,从牧场到野地,
  洪亮又归于沉寂,就好比
在我和那钟声之间关起一道门:

每套四响的钟声各自在风中变奏,
  时而飞扬,时而低沉,
  安宁和友善,友善和安宁,
安宁和友善,送到每个人的心头。

这一年我睡去醒来都是疼痛,
  我几乎盼望着不再醒来,
  盼望这苟延残喘的生命早日停摆,
不要再听到下一次圣诞的钟声:

* 这首诗,和接下来几首诗,描写的是哈勒姆去世后的第一个圣诞节。
† 指四个村庄的四个教堂所各自奏出的四套钟声,每套钟声四响一组,表示安宁与友善。

而正是这钟声接管我动荡不安的心灵，
　　因为孩童时的我就曾被它们掌控；
　　它们带给我饱含喜悦的悲痛，
那是圣诞季节愉快醉人的钟声。

二十九

以这样不可抗拒的理由去悲嗟,
　　当那一日报纸惊扰日常的平安,
　　又封存失去他的遗憾,
我们怎敢继续我们的圣诞夜;

它又怎能带来一个更受欢迎的客人?
　　好令这个夜晚更值得期待,
　　好在歌舞、游戏和嬉闹之间
把无尽欢乐如同礼物一般散开?

但还是去吧,当冬青树的树枝
　　缠绕住寒冷的洗礼池,
　　去依据习俗惯例多做一顶花冠,
好护卫住房屋的大门。

过往时日的老姐妹*,
　　灰发的看护,不喜欢新的事物;
　　但既然她们总归会消亡,
凭什么要她们现在就错失岁贡?

* "老姐妹"和下一行的"灰发看护",都是喻指前一句里的 Use and Wont,即习俗和传统。

三十

用颤抖的手指我们在编织
　　环绕圣诞炉火的冬青；
　　大地上乌云横行，
我们的平安夜忧伤地降临。

如往年一样，我们在客厅小聚，
　　嬉戏打闹，强颜欢笑，
　　但每个人都心怀敬畏地觉察到
有个幽影无声地注视着一切。

我们停下来：风在山毛榉上：
　　我们听见它们正扫荡冬天的土地；
　　而在一个手拉手的圆圈里
我们沉默端坐，相互凝望。

于是我们的声音彼此回荡；
　　我们唱歌，尽管眼神黯淡，
　　去年此时，我们曾和他相伴
唱愉快的歌：我们纵情歌唱：

歌声停顿：一种温柔的感觉蔓延

　　在我们中间：休息是多么合适：

　　"他们休息，"我们说，"他们的睡眠香甜"，

沉默袭来，我们哭泣。

我们的歌声抵达更高的音域；

　　再一次我们唱道："他们没有死

　　没有丧失与人世间的感应，

对我们来说毫无变化，尽管他们已改变；

"聚集起力量，从变幻和脆弱中

　　摆脱，再用这样的力量，

　　这六翼天使般强烈而纯洁的光，

刺穿一圈圈天体，一层层面纱。"

上升，快乐的晨曦，上升，神圣的晨曦，

　　从夜晚唤起欢乐的白昼：

　　哦天父，请轻触东方，擦亮

那希望萌生时微微闪动的光。

三十一

> * Charnel cave,存骸窟,和墓穴不同。按犹太人传统,遗体先在此存放数年,待天然地腐朽之后,家人再来拾取未朽烂的骨头,埋葬到墓穴。

当拉撒路离开存骸窟*,
　　返回到玛利亚的家中,
　　他曾被问道——是否曾渴望
听见她在他墓畔的悲哭?

"兄弟,那四天你在哪里?"
　　而他关于死后情景的回复
　　那必将在赞美之上又增赞美的记录,
并不曾流传下来。

邻人们从家中走出来相见,
　　街道上欢乐声沸腾,
　　一种庄严的愉快甚至达臻
橄榄山紫色的峰巅。

瞧,基督曾令一个人复活!
　　唯有他有幸经受过天启;
　　但他说不出什么;或是
某物封住了福音书作者的唇。

三十二

她眼里住满无声的崇敬,
　　心里容不下别的意念,
　　但,他曾是死者,然后他坐在那里,
带他回来的那个人也坐在那里。

而一种深爱取代了
　　其余的一切,当她的热烈目光
　　游走在兄弟活生生的脸庞,
并落在真生命之上。

所有微妙的想法,所有好奇的敬畏,
　　已被喜悦全然压倒,
　　她屈身,抹救世主的脚
用极贵的香膏,用泪水。

三重赐福给那些虔诚祈祷的生命,
　　给那些在更高的爱中得以持久的爱者;
　　什么样的灵魂可以如此纯粹自足,
或也能像他们这样蒙受幸福?

三十三[*]

[*] 这首诗依旧和拉撒路的故事有关。作者设想姐弟两人,弟弟是经受种种怀疑主义的辛劳与风暴才找到信仰,而姐姐则听从自小受到的教义来自然拥有信仰。这两种信仰之路,在作者看来是可以平行的。

哦,在辛劳和风暴之后的你
  似已抵达一种更纯粹的处境,
  你的信仰随物赋形,
不会委身于形式的铁律,

你的姐姐在祈祷,不要去打搅
  她儿时的天堂,有关幸福的观念;
  也不要用晦涩的暗示去扰乱
她在美妙岁月里的生活。

她依赖仪式的信仰,也和你一般纯粹,
  她的双手更快地触摸到善:
  哦,那酒与饼是神圣的,
她将之与神圣的真理相连!

你瞧,倘若你期望理性
  是在对内在良知的坚守中成熟,
  那么即便缺失了此种预像[†],
你也不会在罪人的世界中沉沦,

[†] Type,指前段所提到的 the flesh and blood,基督的象征。

三十四

我微茫黯淡的此生应当给予我的教诲,
    是生命将存在直至永远,
    否则地球的中心就是黑暗,
到处都是尘土和炉灰;

否则,这绿色的圆,发光的天体*,   * 绿色的圆,指地
    不可思议的美丽,就不过是深埋在   球;发光的天体,
    魔性诗人心里的幻梦,他执笔逞才,   指太阳。
却无关道德也毫无目的。

而在这样的世界中上帝何为?
    倘若一切都是必死之物,如何值得
    再花费时间拣选,也不值得
教人在死前保持些许的耐心;

那最好就是立刻坠向平静,
    像那被魅惑之蛇所攫住的飞鸟,
    一头朝下沦入
空虚黑暗之口,消失殆尽。

三十五

然而,要是某个可让人信任的声音
　自狭窄的墓穴中传来低语,
　"他们面颊耷拉;身体蜷曲;
他们这些死者,在尘土中毫无希望":

我难道不该表示抗议,"即便在此地,
　哪怕只剩片刻,哦爱神,我当尽力
　让如此甜美之物存活。"
我难道非得掉转耳朵,去谛听

那从此无家可归的海的呻吟,
　听那溪流如何或快或慢地侵蚀
　永恒的群山,那陆地沉浮
渐渐变为飞扬的尘土;

听爱也发出叹息的回声,
　"忘川之滨的声响
　会一再摧折我的甜美,
于半死不活中觉察自己将消失。"

哦,这种虚无,对我而言又有何益?
　　倘若死亡就是真的死亡
　　爱就不如从未有过,
或只限于最狭义的此生,

只流于某种无所用心的陪伴,
　　或沦为最粗俗的萨提尔式的肉欲,
　　嚼着香草,榨着美酒,
在林中晒着太阳,饱食终日。

三十六

尽管人们能隐隐感知的那些真理
　　原本扎根于我们自身神秘的构造，
　　我们仍把全部的祝福给予那个名字，
是基督，令那些真理广为流传；

因为智慧是要处理凡人的心智，
　　他们无力感知最浅显词语所表述的真理，
　　而当真理化身为故事，
它将迈进那些贫穷卑微的门槛。

因此，那最初的言*已具呼吸，
　　且在至善至美的行动中
　　以人子之手实践信经中的信经，
这比所有诗性的思想都更有力；

这些事迹，能够令那些庄稼汉、泥瓦匠，
　　抑或掘墓者，都有所感悟，
　　就连那些在围绕珊瑚礁的涛声中望着
海雾的蛮族†的眼睛，也能读懂。

* 指《约翰福音》的开头，"太初有言，言与神同在，言就是神"。

† 指太平洋群岛上的原始部族。

三十七

女神乌拉尼亚*蹙着眉头说道：　　　　　　* 弥尔顿召唤过
　"你何必在你无知的领域喋喋不休，　　　　　的天堂的缪斯，
　　论起信仰，有很多更为纯正的教士，　　　曾引领他上天
也有很多比你更具说服力的声音。　　　　　　入地。

"请沿着你天性的小溪一路下行，
　　在属于你的帕纳塞斯山驻足，
　　听你的月桂树发出甜蜜的私语
拂过群山流转的岩层。"

而我的墨尔波墨涅女神[†]也做出回复，　　　† 悲剧和挽歌的
　　伴随一阵涌上她面颊的羞愧：　　　　　　缪斯。
　　"我当然配不上言说
你那高高在上的神秘；

"因为我只是尘世的缪斯，
　　只拥有一点微薄的技艺，
　　就是用歌声平复疼痛的心灵，
再给予人类之爱以应有的回报；

"但我无法忘怀一位亲爱的死者,

　　以及他对所有神圣事物的言说,

　　（他所说的一切之于我

宛如圣酒之于垂死者那般珍贵）

"我呢喃的,是从显现的真理中紧抓住的

　　安慰,仿佛他就在我身边;

　　就让我在主的葡萄园*游荡一会吧,

且将神圣的真理蒙上歌的面纱。"

* 参见《马太福音》第 20 章,"因为天国好像家主清早出门,雇人进他的葡萄园作工"。

三十八

我拖着疲惫的步伐四处漫游,
　　却总在没有你的天空下,
　　远处绯红色的光辉湮灭了,
我期待的景象和境界荡然无存。

这开花的季节虽不能带来欢乐,
　　不能带来报春的旋律,
　　但在我爱唱的众多歌曲中
似有一丝堪可慰藉的微光。

如果那些获得自由的魂灵
　　尚存留一丝对于此地的关切,
　　那么我要唱给你的这些歌,
就不会完全徒劳,就会被你听见。

三十九

这些地下骸骨的老守卫,
    我随意轻击,你便答之以
    会结果的云,能生育的烟;
幽暗的紫杉,抓紧那碑石,

向着无梦的头颅深深屈膝,
    你也曾有过黄金般的时光,
    当花儿正相互探寻,
悲伤女神——却凝视着死者,

令人类幽暗的墓地变得更暗,——
    她说谎的嘴唇又在低语着什么?
    令你忧郁的枝梢忽然闪亮,
随即又再度陷入忧郁。

四十

但愿我们摆脱未亡人的身份
  来观看从肉体中呼散出的灵,
  像观看一个步入婚典的少女
当她第一次佩戴橘色的花冠!

当她在声声祝福中起身,
  终于离开自己的家,
  就会有希望和轻微的遗憾,
令她娇嫩双眸蒙上四月的无常;

父亲并非真的欢喜,
  眼泪布满母亲的脸颊,
  他们长久地拥抱,道别,
随后她进入另一种爱的领域;

那儿她的职责是去养育,去教导,
  按照合适的方式,
  成为日常的一个环节,
并承接起世代的相继;

而毫无疑问地，是你
　　同样被许以结出不朽果实的生命，
　　在那些伟大的、相称于
天堂成熟活力的职责中。

唉，对于我，这差异自当有所辨识！
　　她先前的家庭将时常
　　为新娘的音信而感到愉快，
她也将时常可以归宁，

跟他们述说那些他们愿意听的事务，
　　把孩子带来，夸耀他，
　　直到那些最想念她的人都将接受
她新的状态，如出嫁前一样可爱：

但你和我已然握手告别，
　　直到好些个冬天令我躺下；
　　我的路在我熟悉的田野，
而你的路，是在未被发现的大陆。

四十一

在我们不可避免的丧失之前,你的精神
　　的确不断地从高处升向更高处;
　　如同朝向天空的爱的火焰,
如更轻盈者飞越芸芸众生。

但你被转向一些陌生的事物,
　　而我已失去那些联结你变化的
　　纽带;我只能在此,在大地之上,
无法再参与你的变化。

多么荒唐!然而可能就是这样——
　　我曾尽力鼓舞起意志
　　去跃过生命与光的等级,
飞闪到你身边,我的朋友。

因为尽管我的天性很少会屈服于
　　蕴藏在死亡里的不确定的恐惧;
　　也不会临渊战栗于
那从忘川传来的嚎叫和哭泣;

然而很多时候,当落日环绕荒野,
    我审视内心的烦恼,发觉
    我将不再是你的友伴,
这种幽灵似的疑虑使我寒冷,

纵使我,以上升的心智
    跟随那些降临在你身上的奇迹,
    不停穿越所有的来世,
也始终无法赶上你,无法一起生活。

四十二

一种晦暗的幻觉烦扰着我的心:
　　他在赛跑中仍将我甩在身后;
　　只因我们属于同一个地方,
才让我梦想着与他并列。

那么,愿天地让我们保持如此,
　　愿他,这被深爱的,
　　这拥有丰富经验的,
再度培育出成熟的心智与意志:

什么样的欢乐能抗衡
　　那样搅动深心的欢乐,
　　当一个人爱着却一无所知,
却从那爱与全知者处收获真理?

四十三

如果睡眠与死亡确为一体,
  每一颗心灵所闭合的花瓣都将沉睡,
  在一些漫长的恍惚状态里
越过生命轮回中的全部幽暗;

失去肉体的心灵
  难以意识到时间的流逝,
  而往昔未被记载的踪迹
也将会融入花朵不断变化的色泽中:

那么对人类而言就没有什么会失去;
  所以,那灵魂的寂静花园
  布满图案缤纷的花瓣,它们记载了
有生命以来的整个尘世;

而爱将持续,纯粹而完整
  如他在这短暂时空中给予我的爱,
  并将随着曙光中的灵魂一同苏醒
在又一个精神世界的起点。

四十四

随幸福的死而发生的是什么?
　　此处,死者日益强大,
　　而他遗忘了过往的生活,
上帝合上他头顶的囟门。

音调和色彩,已随时光消逝,
　　然而囤积的感觉或许
　　偶尔迸发(他不知道来自何处)
一些闪光,一点神秘暗示;

在漫长而和谐的岁月里
　　(如果死者确已品尝忘川之水),
　　愿人世间的微茫气息
令正与同伴偕行的你惊奇。

倘若这样一种梦幻的感觉降临,
　　哦,请你转过身来,请打消这怀疑;
　　我的守护天使将自那高处
朗声告诉你所有的过去。

四十五

这婴儿初来到世间,
    每当他将柔嫩的手掌
    伸向自己的胸脯,
他还从未思考过:"这就是我。"

但随着他长大,集聚经验,
    并学习区分主格和宾格的"我",
    然后发现"我并不是我之所见,
也异于我所触碰之物"。

由此,他转向一个独立的心智
    从此清晰的意识或会开启,
    正如通过那个束缚他的形体
他也渐渐界定出一个孤单的自我。

血肉与呼吸能担负的不过如此
    其他的责任皆是徒劳,
    倘若人们不得不重新自我学习,
在死所带来的第二次诞生之后。

四十六

我们正沿着这条渐低的小路下行,
  我们曾经过的道路,荆棘和花束,
  渐次隐没在时辰的阴影中,
好让生活得以一直向前。

就这样吧:而那死后深沉的黎明里
  将不会再有类似的阴影,
  从地平线的一端到另一端
永恒的过往将清晰地呈现;

一生的轨迹被揭示;
  静静增长的果实累累的时日;
  光阴有序,一片丰饶的安宁,
而其中蕴藏最最珍贵的五年*。

哦,爱神,你曾统治的范围并不广阔,
  一块有限的且无法再拓展的领土,
  爱神,你这徘徊不去的星,用玫红色的温暖
照耀我,从地平线的一端到另一端。

---

* 指哈勒姆和丁尼生共同在剑桥度过的大学生活,从 1828 年至 1833 年。

四十七

每个看起来各自独立的灵魂,
　　将在它的轨道上运转,并再度
　　把自我的边界统统消融,随后将坠落,
汇入浩瀚浑茫的总体式的灵魂。

无论信仰是否含混如所有的不堪:
　　永恒的形体仍会从一切灵魂中
　　拣选出永恒的灵魂*,
而当我们相遇时我将认出他:

我们将在无尽的宴席中坐下,
　　相互享受彼此的善:
　　是什么样恢弘的梦能忍心刺伤
那在尘世属于爱神的柔情?他寻找,至少

在最后的和最尖锐的高处†,
　　在我们的灵逐渐消散之前,
　　在靠岸处‡,他寻求一个拥抱和道别:
"珍重!我们把自我弃绝在光中。"

* 指那些在末日审判时复活的荣耀身体中仍能暂时保留个体性的灵魂。

† 个体生命的顶端,从此处,灵魂将坠入永恒的海洋,不复再有个体性的存在。

‡ 在那里,两个灵魂会最后一次相遇,在失去各自的个性并将各自的灵魂融入灵魂总体的海洋之前。

四十八

如果这些源于悲哀的,简短诗行,
    被当作诸如封闭而
    严肃的问答,如此处所提供的,
那么人们也许会对之报以轻蔑:

悲哀所在意的不是剖析与证明;
    当更狂暴的情绪缓和,她任凭
    一丝丝怀疑的阴影在心底游走,
并最终使之都臣服于爱:

因此,真的,她玩弄言辞,
    却进一步服务于健全的律法,
    认为从心弦上奏出动人曲调
是罪与羞耻:

她岂敢信任太长的诗行,
    而是宁可从唇边放纵
    欲言又止的短歌,将翅膀
蘸取泪水,又轻轻掠过。

四十九

艺术，自然以及学派，
　　听凭它们随意的影响闪过，
　　像许多颤动着的鱼叉上的寒光
搅动斑驳的池塘：

思想最轻的波动将难以把握，
　　幻觉最弱的涟漪散开，
　　歌声最细微的呼吸将会
使沉闷的表面泛起波纹。

顺着你的目光搜寻，走你自己的路，
　　但你不要去责备风
　　那令死水荡出涟漪的风，
那用柔软铅笔写就的影戏。

在所有幻觉的希望与恐惧下方，
　　唉，我的悲哀潜入深底
　　咽喑而行，将我生活的根基
淹没在泪水中。

五十

靠近我，当我已至暮年，
　　当血气懈惰，神经感觉刺痛，
　　耳鸣阵阵；心也总是沉重，
那存在的车轮全都放缓。

靠近我，当感官的肉身
　　被压垮信心的剧痛所折磨；
　　而时间，一个挥撒尘土的疯人，
而生活，一位喷火的复仇女神。

靠近我，当我的信仰干枯，
　　而人们，那些暮春的飞蝇，
　　已产下了卵，嘤嘤嗡嗡
编织他们小小的牢房，再死去。

靠近我，当我临终之际，
　　指给我看人类斗争的终点，
　　在生命低暗的边缘，
指给我看永恒之日的晨曦。

五十一

我们当真渴求死者
　应该仍然在我们这边紧挨着我们?
　难道没有什么我们要隐藏的怯懦?
难道没有我们惧怕的内在卑劣?

我曾努力博取他的掌声,
　也曾敬畏于他的责难,
　他清澈的眼眸会察觉我隐藏的羞耻么?
我是否会在他的爱里一点点变轻?

我因不真实的恐惧误解了死亡:
　爱将因缺乏信念而受到责备吗?
　伟大的死亡必有智慧:
死者会洞悉我的一切。

靠近我们,当我们攀登或跌落:
　你们观看,像上帝,翻滚的时日
　用比我们更辽阔的另一种眼睛,
给我们所有人以体谅。

五十二

我无力按我当尽的本分那样爱你，
　　因为爱自当体现所爱之物；
　　而我的诗句徒有言辞，
就是这些思想顶端的泡沫。

"请你不要责备你的这些哀伤的歌，"
　　真爱的魂灵回答道；
　　"你不可能将我从你那边移走，
人类的弱点也无法有损于我。"

"有什么能维持一种精神始终不渝地
　　追随他所企怀的典范？
　　有史可稽么？就连在叙利亚晴空下[*]
人子的无罪岁月也难以做到：

"因此别像一个无所事事的少女，
　　忧愁于生命受罪孽的挫灭，
　　忍耐：你的财富满盈，
当时间从贝壳中褪出珍珠。"

[*] 暗指《圣经》里对耶稣生平的记载。

五十三

我曾看见多少个父亲
  成为儿女绕膝的稳重男子,
  他的青春充满愚蠢的喧嚣,
却又健康安然地度过成年:

而我们岂敢屈服于这样的幻象:
  若非撒落在地里的野燕麦*,
  田地就全然贫瘠,就难以长出
供人活命的粮食?

或者,即便那些经受住青春烈焰的生命
  令我们曾信服这样的学说,
  然而面对旋转不息的恶的涡流,
又岂可将它作为一个真理宣扬?

持有你的善:划出清晰的界限:
  以免神圣的哲学
  将逾越她的领域,并成为
地狱上议院的老鸨。

---

* 野燕麦是危害青稞等农作物的农田恶性杂草之一。作者在这里用野燕麦比喻恶的力量,隐含着对歌德《浮士德》中梅菲斯特"善恶一体论"的批评,梅菲斯特说,"我是总想作恶、却总行了善的那种力量的一部分"。

五十四

我们仍旧相信,以某种方式
　　善将成为恶不可更改的终点,
　　无论本性的折磨,意志的罪孽,
抑或信仰的危机,肉欲的侵蚀;

相信万事俱有其目标;
　　相信没有生命会被毁坏
　　会被当作垃圾投向虚空,
当上帝完成了他的工作;

相信没有一条虫豸被白白劈开,
　　没有一只飞蛾带着徒然的渴求
　　皱缩于徒劳的烈火,
或是仅仅成全他人的利益;

瞧,我们一无所知,
　　我只能相信善终将降临
　　在最后——遥远的——终端,降临于众生,
而每个冬天都会变为春天。

我这样梦想着：但我是什么？
　　一个婴孩在黑夜里哭喊：
　　一个婴孩哭求着光明，
没有语言，唯有哭泣。

五十五

这愿望,是对于全部生者的愿望,
　　祝愿他们的生命不会被坟墓所终止,
　　它难道不是来自我们心底
灵魂最接近上帝的部分?

那么上帝和自然势必争斗吗?
　　为这自然竟助长这等恶魔的梦。
　　她似乎只在意物种,
毫不在乎个体的生命;

于是我四处探究,深思
　　她行为中的秘义,
　　发现她时常繁衍出无数的种子
却只令一个能够存活,

我蹒跚在我曾坚定行走之处,
　　被我思虑的重量拖倒
　　在这宏伟世界的祭坛之阶上,
那斜斜的台阶穿过黑暗通向上帝,

我伸出残损的信仰之手,摸索,
　　聚集尘灰与糠秕,呼唤
　　我所感觉到的,万有的主,
柔弱地相信那更大的希望。

五十六

"我只在意物种么?"并不!
　于岩层和化石中,自然界叫喊道,
　"千万物种已经灭绝:
我才不在乎,一切都将湮灭。

"汝等呼求告泣于我,
　我使万物生长,我令它们消亡,
　灵魂不过意味着呼吸,
我所知的唯有这些。"然后他出现,

作为人,自然界最后的作品,如此美丽,
　他眼中闪烁如此辉煌的意图,
　把圣歌送上寒冷的天穹,
建造他徒劳祈祷的神庙,

他相信上帝就是绝对的爱
　而爱是造物最后的法则——
　尽管大自然,爪牙沾满鲜血,
在深谷中,尖叫着反对他的教义——

他爱过,受过无尽痛苦,

 他曾奋力要为真理和正义而战,

 就是这样的人,却一定要被吹散成沙尘,

或被封在铁丘陵之内?

再也没有了?继而一个怪物,一个梦,

 一个不谐和音。原初的龙族

 在泥浆中彼此的撕裂,

与之相比也是曼妙柔音,

生命如灯心草篓般微不足道!

 唉,但愿有你安慰和祝福的声音!

 答案或补救的希望何在?

在帷幕之后,在帷幕之后。

五十七

请安心地离开吧 *：这悲哀的歌   * 这首诗的口吻
    终究是尘世的歌：   可能是丁尼生
    请安心地离开吧：这样任性的歌   设想一封写给
是对他的不义：让我们走吧。   妹妹的信。

来；让我们走吧：你的面颊苍白；
    而我的半生遗落身后：
    我以为我的朋友会在这诗句中不朽；
但我终将是过客；我这工作也将失败。

然而只要听觉尚存，我们这些人的耳朵里
    就会有一整套缓缓敲响的钟声
    仿佛在宣告那最甜美灵魂的消逝，
那灵魂曾拥有一双人性的眼睛观看。

此刻我听见钟声从四面八方传来
    这是对于死者的永恒祝愿；
    它说着"珍重，珍重，珍重"，
"再见啊，再见"，直到永远。

五十八

我用这些悲哀的诗句作为告别:
  像幽冥殿堂里的回声,
  像水一滴一滴地落在
地下墓室里,它们滴落;

犹在滴落,毫无意义地击碎
  终日跳动的平静心灵,
  他们垂死肉身已半入黄土,
他们将消失于寒冷的地窖。

缪斯乌拉尼亚回答道:"为何一再
  用徒劳的泪水悲悼你的同胞?
  请在此地稍作忍受,
你将以一种更高贵的方式离开。"

五十九

哦悲哀,你若是决意要与我同居,
  请不要作为短暂的情人,而是作为妻子,
  作为我的密友以及生命另一半;
因为我承认这势必如此;

哦悲哀,你若是决意掌管我的血气,
  偶尔可以如新娘般可爱;
  但请抛开你更为峻厉的情绪,
如果你决意赐我明智与善。

我聚集的热情既不会更移,
  也不会从此刻开始减少;
  但我将偶尔有写诗的借口,
因为由爱而生的悲哀萦绕着我;

大声宣告你的存在,因你是我的,
  伴随如此强烈的对于未来的希望,
  希望无论如何我都能了解你,
而有些人可能还难于叫出你的名字。

六十

他走了；风姿卓绝的灵魂：
  我仍一如既往地爱他，
  像那些贫苦的女孩心系着
高门贵第中的情人。

他与适合他的环境打成一片，
  而她发觉自己如此卑微，
  她半是嫉妒于她所不懂的事物，
又妒忌在他身旁的一切。

小小的村庄看起来绝望孤寂，
  她在局促的时日里叹息忧郁，
  围着家务事转来转去，
在那座她出生的灰暗房子里。

愚蠢的邻居经过，
  取笑她，直至暮色昏茫，
  在夜晚她哭泣，"我是多么虚妄！
他怎会爱如此低微的我？"

六十一

如果,在你庄严超群的第二形态中,
    你被解放的头脑与之交谈的
      是全部智者的群体,
人类社会中完美的花朵;

而如果你向下俯瞰,
    将见到怎样纤弱和模糊的品性,
      寒冷和夜晚的增长是怎样无足轻重,
我注定在黑暗中变得怎样苍白!

但是,请把目光再转向这模糊的海岸[*],
    你最初呈现为一个男人形体的地方,
      我爱过你,就连
莎士比亚[†]的灵魂也不能爱你更多。

[*] 指地球,从哈勒姆现在所在的天堂位置看过去,只是隐约可见。
[†] 暗指莎士比亚写给友人的那些十四行情诗。

六十二

然而如果你投注于我的目光所看到的
 　　使你生出几分退缩或犹移,
 　　那么我的爱就是一个无意义的故事,
是属于过去的褪色传奇;

而你,如同一个曾屈尊错爱的人,
 　　当他还只是一个轻衣少年,
 　　曾和一些不相称的心灵厮混,
但最终是要与一个同等的心智结合;

他呼吸一个新世界的空气,同时
 　　他其他的激情全都消亡,
 　　或者按照更为深刻的眼光,
那些激情只是些一笑置之的小事。

六十三

在我的心朝着天堂上升的过程中,
  对于胯下被驱策的马儿的怜悯,
  以及对于被猎犬撕碎的猎物的爱,
并不能占据多少的分量;

我远远高于这些可怜的动物,
  正如你可能也远远高于我,
  而我不只是要怜悯它们,
我也想抚慰它们的痛苦。

因此,当我伫立哭泣,请你看着我,
  尽管,你身不由己地进入更广阔的运动,
  环行在属于你的轨道上,
朝向更高的高天,更深的深渊。

六十四

你可回顾一路走过的征尘,
　　像一位天资卓越的男子,
　　他的生活起于微细,
在乡下的田间地里长成;

他打破不公平的出身瓶颈,
　　抓住幸运女神的裙裳,
　　逆环境的险恶而上,
努力克服自己讨厌的命运;

他依靠强力传扬自己的价值,
　　活着抓住那金制钥匙,
　　去打造一个强权国度的法令,
并左右着来自王座的私语;

他在命运的斜坡上攀登,
　　升至登峰造极的位置,
　　成为民众期待的栋梁,
走向世人仰慕的中心;

然而如同置身于沉思的梦里,
　　当他整个人放松下来,
　　就仍感觉到山陵中遥远的爱,
溪水中隐密的甜美,

那是他往昔狭窄的一方天地,
　　在那潺潺流淌的泉水边,
　　他和一个最早的伙伴,
玩过大臣和国王的游戏;

这伙伴辛苦开垦自己的田地,
　　依靠双手获得一份收成,
　　他抑或会站在犁沟里沉思凝想,
"我的老朋友能记得我吗?"

六十五

亲爱的灵魂,请照你自己的心意来对待我,
　　面对胡思乱想掀起的困扰,我劝慰自己,
　　"爱是珍贵到不可能失去,
一丁点谷粒也不会洒出。"

在那样的慰藉中我方能歌唱,
　　直到熬过自我怀疑的痛苦,
　　一种幸福的思想呼之欲出
把自身的平衡系于轻盈的翅膀:

既然我们够得上朋友这个称谓,
　　你因此一直在我里面活着,
　　而我的一部分也会在你里面活着
随你前往神圣的终端。

六十六

你曾以为我的心已满是疮痍,
　　因此当我着迷于人群欢乐的幻景,
　　像一个为琐事欢愉的流民,
你会困惑于我这样的行迹。

我生命已然蒙上的阴影,
　　在心里形成一块荒地,
　　使我对同类充满柔情,
使我近似于一个失明的人;

他被牵引着穿过庭院,
　　在朋友间随意谑浪,
　　他让孩子们坐在膝上,
用手抚弄他们的发卷:

他翻着花绳,他敲打座椅
　　只图消遣,同时又梦想着天空,
　　他深藏的往昔从未消亡,
他的丧失之夜始终在那里。

六十七

当月光洒在我床前,
  我知道在你栖息的地方,
  紧挨着西面辽阔的河流,
同样有道光辉正映于墙面;

在黑暗中闪亮的是你的碑石,
  当缓缓流淌的银色光束
  拂过你姓名的每一个字母,
又拂过你生卒年月的数字。

那神秘的光辉转瞬即逝,
  月光也从我床头退散,
  于是我闭紧疲惫的眼睑,
一直睡到夜色里浸透了晨曦:

然后我知道雾已经给整个国土
  都蒙上透明的轻纱,
  你的碑板闪烁,向着黎明,
黑暗教堂中的一个幽灵。

六十八

当我蜷缩在羽绒枕被里,
　　睡眠,死之孪生兄弟,请调匀我的呼吸,
　　睡眠,死之孪生兄弟,对死一无所知,
我梦见的你也不会是一个死者:

我如从前一般孑孓而行,
　　当我们走过的小径沾满新露,
　　而大片的筋骨草在微风中
簌簌作响如破晓的晨号。

但这是什么?我再三忖度,
　　在你的眼中我发觉一丝烦忧,
　　它使我悲哀,我不知缘由,
梦也不能消解这疑惑:

但在云雀飞离草地之前,
　　我醒了,领悟到真相,
　　那原是我青春时期的烦忧
被愚蠢的睡眠转移给了你。

六十九

我梦见春天一去不回,
　　自然丧失它古老的力量,
　　霜雾笼罩街巷,
他们倚在门边饶舌:

我漫步离开这嘈杂的市镇,
　　发觉一处荆棘丛生的林丘,
　　我采了荆条围在额头,
就像佩戴了一顶公民花冠:

我所遇皆是嘲笑,皆是蔑视,
　　从孩童、青年到白发翁伯,
　　他们在公共广场唤我,
那个戴着荆棘冠冕的傻子:

他们唤我傻子,将我戏弄,
　　我却找到了一个夜天使,
　　他声音低柔,面色明晰,
看着我的冠冕,现出笑容:

他伸出一只荣耀之手,
　　仿佛要令这荆冠变成绿叶:
　　那声音并不悲切,
那言辞却难猜透。

七十

我不能辨清那面容,
  当我在幽暗中力图绘出
  那张熟悉的脸,那色调模糊
且消融于夜的虚空;

幽灵似的石匠锻造的云塔,
  曾关闭又裂开的深渊,
  一只指引之手,披着斗篷的身影,
晃动在我神思迷离的梦境;

人们从张着大嘴的门中涌出,
  成群结队皱褶的脸闪过,
  一大团黑暗半死不活地翻滚,
在无尽的岸边排着怠惰的长队;*

直到我突然间摆脱了意志,
  听到神奇的音乐升起,
  透过灵魂的晶格
看见你美丽的脸,使我平静。

---

* 这里可参考但丁《神曲》里对地狱入口处的描述。

七十一

睡眠,你这死亡、灵幻与疯狂的
    同族,你终于令过去的欢乐
    在这个夜晚重现,此刻
我们正一起穿过夏日的法兰西;

你在灵魂面前有如此的影响么?
    好吧,来给我三倍剂量的鸦片,
    麻醉那蒙昧的罪感,
以为就此拥有完整无憾的欢乐;

此刻我们如从前一样推心置腹,
    谈论人和心智,尘世变迁,
    光阴荏苒流转,
而我们一如既往地漫步;

越过林木丛生的河畔,
    越过堡垒,起伏的山岗,
    瀑布在桥面溅起闪光,
碎浪摔碎在浅滩。

七十二

<small>* 这一天是哈勒姆逝世一周年，1834 年 9 月 15 日。</small>

阴暗的黎明*，你正以此种方式重现么？
　　你咆哮着，撕开夜的遮盖，
　　带来疾风，把白杨抽刮得灰白，
这疾风夹着暴雨，击打湿漉漉的窗格。

这一天，我的生命从荣耀的顶端
　　转为悲惨，倒退回那个末日，
　　那个令繁花萎谢，
令天地蒙尘的末日；

这一天先是用阵雨开启了
　　悲伤的时刻，阵雨使玫瑰
　　倾欹，又使雏菊紧锁
她深红色的花瓣；

就算天空随后放晴，能在深邃的东方
　　举起平静的火焰，抑或那风变得轻柔，
　　能沿着山陵，操演光与影的变幻，
然而我只觉一切依然，

一样的苍白、寒冷、狂野,犹如此刻,
　　这一天,仿佛被一些可怕的罪孽所铭刻,
　　当黑暗之手穿过时间击倒
并抹去自然的精华:只剩下你,这阴暗的黎明

你将尽力抬起深锁的眉头,
　　越过湿透晨星的云层,
　　你将流云席卷至远方,
又在天空种满飞翔的树枝,

随后你将伴着雷鸣行至拱顶,
　　行至正午时分,灾难性的一天,
　　也终于会熬至暮霭降临,一天将尽,
但愿这一天从此灭没。

七十三

诸多世界,诸多要做的事情,
　　此世的捕风,命定如此,
　　我怎知不是其他世界在需要你?
因你刚强,一如你纯真。

我所预见的属于你的声名已湮灭,
　　头颅错过了尘世的花冠,
　　但我不诅咒自然,也不诅咒死亡,
因为没有事情会偏离自然的法则。

我们只是经过;那条人类生活的小路
　　蔓草丛生,或终归荆榛,
　　在无尽的岁月里,什么样的声名能留给
人类的行为?这取决于上帝。

哦,没落名声的空洞幻影
　　此刻完全褪去,而灵魂狂喜着
　　它努力聚集着大的力量,
这力量才有可能锻造出人类之名。

七十四

在那些执着的观看者眼里,
 死者脸上有时会呈现出
 一种之前难以察觉的
族类的相似:

同样,亲爱的,如今你眉梢已冷,
 我也辨识清楚你之所是,
 明白你与那些已逝的智者相似,
且与古代的大师们同宗。

但还有东西超出我的目力,
 而我看清的地方也欲言又止,
 也不去谈论,因我懂得死神
要用你使他的黑暗美丽。

七十五

在我用来自我安慰的诗行里,
 我不表达对你的赞美,
 仅让人根据我悲痛的程度,
来猜测你的伟大;

选词酌句的作手,
 或音域宽广的歌者,
 他们要具备什么样的体验
才有力量还原你从前的模样?

在这些褪色的日子里,我不打算
 仅仅短暂地哭喊几声,
 也无意把你置入柔曼歌吟,
只给予一点琐碎的赞美。

你的枝叶已在春天里枯萎,
 而我们仍在这片日光下呼吸,
 这个世界只认可已发生的事,
并漠视所有可能发生的事。

于是在此地,沉默将护卫你的名声,
    而在某处,人类视野之外,
    无论你要着手去做什么,
伴随的都是喧腾的欢呼。

七十六

乘着幻想的翅膀,上升,
　　顷刻之间你看见
　　所有繁星密布的诸天
都聚集在一根针的顶端;

乘着预言的翅膀,轻盈穿过
　　无尽现世的深渊,
　　看,在紫杉朽坏之前,
你最强力的诗歌已哑默;

而即便那唤醒我们星球黑暗的
　　最初的晨歌,仍在回荡,
　　这无限空间中,你自己的歌
在橡树长至盛年之前,仍将凋谢。

在这些枝繁叶茂的树荫历经
　　五十个春秋之前,你的歌是徒劳,
　　而当某一天,这些橡树和紫杉变成
中空之塔般的遗迹,它们又是什么?

七十七

有何希望可言？这些现代韵诗。
 　　他将沉思的眼睛转向
 　　诸多诗歌，行动，乃至生活，
它们在时间的深处统统缩略成微茫。

这些凡人的痛苦摇篮曲
 　　会装订成册，会压在箱底，
 　　或用于卷曲少女们的发绺，
或当第一千次月亏发生之际

某个书摊上的人会发现它们，
 　　而后，短暂的，翻过那讲述悲伤的
 　　一页，更换成另一首歌，
来自另一个早被遗忘的心灵。

但那又如何？我渐暗的道路
 　　仍将回荡着音乐；
 　　吐露我的丧失，这比我的名声重要，
说出爱，这胜过一切悦耳的赞美。

七十八

[*] 这是哈勒姆死后的第二个圣诞节。

又是一个圣诞节*,我们
　　用冬青环绕圣诞节的壁炉,
　　沉默的雪笼罩大地,
我们的圣诞夜静静降临:

圣诞柴闪耀冰霜的挽歌,
　　风的羽翼不曾掠过天际,
　　所有事物都睡思昏沉,
在失去某物的平静中。

如以往那些冬日一样,
　　再次祭出我们古老的游戏,
　　模仿画中人逼真的优雅,
再一起跳舞,唱歌和捉迷藏。

谁显露一丝悲苦的征兆?
　　没有一滴泪,没有疼痛的印记:
　　哦忧愁,忧愁也能一点点减少?
哦不幸,不幸亦能渐化作微末?

哦仅剩下遗憾,遗憾也会消灭!

  不——混合所有这些神秘的情绪,

  深处的悲伤一如往昔,

但悲伤的泪水长久流淌,已然干枯。

七十九

"这已经超出了手足的情谊,"——
　　让这不要再烦扰你,高贵的心!
　　我了解,是何种力量使你
拥有最昂贵的完整的爱。

但你和我是同一种人,
　　宛如自然的铸币厂所铸造,
　　而山林和田野把同样甜美的形态
印在我们彼此的心智中。

对于我们,同样寒冷的溪流蜿蜒
　　穿过所有旋涡涌动的峡谷,同样的
　　所有漫游在薄暮中的风
一起融合为这美丽世界的低语。

我们簇拥在同一个亲爱的膝边起誓,
　　从同一本书中习得同一种课程,
　　随后,我们童年的亚麻色卷发慢慢变成
棕色和黑色,在同宗同族的额头之上。

因此我和你拥有相似的财富,
　　但在他丰盈之地,我是贫乏,
　　他与我的不同之处
恰好使他弥补我的欠缺。

八十

倘若说有什么朦胧的愿望,
　　那么我愿意在亚瑟死之前
　　就让神圣的死神仁慈地把我带走,
把尘土洒在我无泪的双眼之上;

然后竭尽全力,想象
　　失去我这件事情给他所造成的悲痛,
　　一种与生命或思想同等深度的悲痛,
却还能维系住神人之间的安宁。

我头脑中有一幅画面闪烁,
　　我听见他说出的那些词句,
　　他忍受周而复始的重负,
但把重负都转化为收获。

他的榜样令我得以自由,
　　得以深刻地被安慰,被拯救,
　　这未曾实践的典范,从坟墓中
伸出死者的手抚慰我。

八十一

当他活着的时候,但愿我曾说过,
　"我的爱此刻将不再游移,
　不再有更为醇美的变化,
因为此刻爱就是成熟的谷穗。"

然而,爱却也曾期待更丰富的贮藏:
　我的抱怨到底能有什么结果?
　"更多的岁月会使我更加爱你。"
这萦绕于心的低语使我晕眩。

但死报之以一个甜蜜的答案:
　"我突然的霜冻是意外的收获,
　令谷物得以完全地成熟,
它或许已汲取了余烬中的热量。"

八十二

我不会和死神有任何争执
　　为在形体和面孔上产生的变化,
　　他与尘土所孕育的更为低级的生命
也不能摇动我的信念。

永恒之路不辞迢递,
　　精神在不断蜕变中上升,
　　而这些变化本身不过是被粉碎的秸秆,
或是被打破的蛹茧。

我不谴责死亡,是因为他将德性的作用
　　传送到尘世之外,
　　我知道被迁移的人类价值
在别处也会开花结果。

我向死神发泄心头积存的怒火,
　　仅仅是因为
　　他令我们的生命分隔得这么远,
让我们不能听见彼此的言说。

八十三

请降临在这北方的海滨,
　哦甜美的迟迟未至的新岁月;
　你辜负了期盼中的自然,
迟迟未至,不可再迟。

什么能把你拦阻在多云的正午之外?
　什么能拒绝你的芬芳入驻它的领地?
　烦恼焉能与四月的日子并驰,
而夏季的月份怎可容有悲哀?

请带来红门兰,带来毛地黄的嫩芽,
　小小婆婆纳可爱的蓝,
　露水烧灼的深郁金香,
还有金链花那倒垂的火焰。

哦,新的岁月,你迟迟未至,
　阻滞了我血液中的哀思,
　它渴望迸放凝霜的蓓蕾
让更清新的喉咙涌出歌声。

八十四

每当我独自一人,沉思细想
　　那在地下的你原本要度过的一生,
　　我思想你的新月倘若变盈
将怎样通体散发灼热的辉光;

我看见你满载着善坐在那里,
　　如同一个温暖流荡的中心,
　　在一瞥一笑间,在握手和亲吻中,
向你所有的亲人散发幸福的热力;

你的亲人,某种程度上,也是我的;
　　因为那一刻佳期就要临近,
　　你将把你的生活与我的一位家人
紧紧相连,而你的孩子们

会在我的膝边唤我"舅舅";
　　但那个铁一般残酷无情的日子
　　使她的橙花变成了柏枝,
让希望落空,你化为坟丘。

我想必能满足他们最细小的愿望,
　　拍他们的脸颊,视为己出。
　　我看见他们从未出生的脸庞发亮
在你从未点起的炉火旁。

我看见自己是一个受尊敬的客人,
　　是你绚丽的文学道路上的伙伴,
　　一起在餐桌前亲切交谈,
或热烈辩论,再开一些优雅的玩笑;

而此刻你丰饶的创作也会赢得
　　人们异口同声的真心赞美,
　　幸福的白昼,日复一日,
在金色的山陵间合上帷幕,

又许诺下另一个同样美好的清晨;
　　那些丰盈的岁月的车辙
　　穿过一条条积聚力量的道路,
令你成为一位备受尊崇的老人;

直到这灵魂的尘世外衣穿至破旧,
　　她丰富的使命也得以完成,

留下恢弘的思想遗产，你的灵魂
随后将从这个星球消逝远走；

那也是我的灵魂可以逃走的时辰，
　　因为爱和命运将我们的灵魂相连，
　　在这忧伤的海峡上空久久盘旋，
再与你融合，一起去往彼岸，

最后抵达那神圣的终端，
　　那个曾在圣地赴死的人子
　　会用发光的手接引我们，
把我们当成单个完整的灵魂。

我所斜倚的是什么样的芦苇？
　　啊，对往日的设想，为什么
　　再次唤醒这陈旧的苦涩，
打破了刚刚获得的一点平静。

八十五

当我哀恸最甚之时，我领悟
  这从棺架与柩衣中孕育的真理，
  宁可爱过又失去
也不愿从未爱过*——

* 参见第 27 首第 13—16 行。

这言辞的真理，已经受行动的考验，
  要追问，并以此安慰
  我们生命中这共同的悲痛，
追问我所过的是何种生活；

是否，我对天上事物所寄予的信任，
  会因悲痛而减弱，抑或，一如既往；
  是否，对他的爱已经耗尽
我所拥有的爱的能力；

你†的言辞感人至深，
  凭借轻柔的责备，含蓄的表达，
  以及对于宽容律法的忠诚。
它发自肺腑，让人信赖。

† 这里的"你"，是指丁尼生的另一位好友埃德蒙·勒欣顿，他日后（1842 年）娶了丁尼生的另一位妹妹塞西莉亚。这首诗大约是诗人在勒欣顿新婚之时写给他的。

在听到他死讯之前,
　　我的心气保持笃定的基调,
　　在维也纳致命的高墙内,
上帝的手指触碰他,他熟睡。

那些卓绝的心智列队而来,
　　在我们凡人国土的上方
　　绕着那神圣之门围成圆圈,
欢迎并接纳他的到来;

领他穿越至福之地,
　　在新鲜的源泉里向他显现
　　血肉之躯在循环的时间中
所积聚的全部知识。

但我留在此地,我的希望渺茫,
　　我的生活,思想,毫无价值,
　　徒然游荡在日益黑暗的大地,
这里所有围绕我的事物都在讲述他。

哦友谊,请用坚定的手掌控我,
　　哦心灵,请用最仁慈的跳动温暖我,

哦神圣的本质，另一种形式，
哦庄严的灵，哦头戴冠冕的魂！

然而没有人能比我更知道
 人类意志的感官会要求
 多少由人类自行做出的举动，
据此，我们敢于生，或敢于死。

无论我的日子怎样衰颓，
 我曾感到，现在也感到，尽管独自留下，
 他存在于我自身的存在里，
他生活的足迹也在我的足迹中；

一种生活，由诸位缪斯慷慨赐予
 优雅的天赋，得以表达
 所有可以理解的温柔，
所有极尽精微的智慧：

因此我的激情并没有屈从于
 软弱，我发现一种安慰心智的
 图景，在我的悲痛中
有一种力量得以保持。

同样地，那想象他人痛苦的能力，
　　使我热爱从事精神性的斗争，
　　并将那震惊贯穿我整个的生命，
但也随之缓解我当下的重创。

我的脉搏因此重新跳动，
　　为着我曾遇见的其他朋友；
　　但这也不会使我忘记
那令我们成为人类的巨大希望。

我恳求你的爱：我认为
　　任何过分的哀悼是有罪的；
　　我，是这样一种已克服时间的友谊
所残存下来的那一半；

这友谊确实克服了时间，它是
　　不朽的，远离恐惧：
　　那收夺一切的岁月
也不能从这里带走部分：

然而，滚烫洪水之上的夏日，
　　以及溢满狭长小溪的春天，

还有在枝叶渐疏的林间聚集的秋天,
伴着白嘴鸦的喧哗,

以及微风和水波的每一次颤动
　　都在光线明暗的变化中回忆,
　　我坟墓里的旧爱,
以及我随之而去的那部分最好的热情:

我坟墓里的旧爱,
　　沉静者中的一员,想要说:
　　"起来,向前去寻找
未来岁月里的友谊。

"我从平静的海岸边看着你;
　　你的灵魂可以触碰到我的灵魂;
　　但在可爱的人类语言的范围内
我们再也无法相互交流。"

而我愿回答说,"尘世的云彩会污染
　　自由世界里繁星密布的清朗吗?
　　这如何可能?对于我的痛苦,
你能生出一种毫无痛苦的共鸣吗?"

那私语随之轻轻地传来：

　"对你而言，参透它有点艰难；

　我在决定性的祝福中凯旋，

一切都有平静的结果。"

我就是这样与死者交谈；

　或设想死者将要说的话；

　悲痛总会敏感于种种的启示，

满怀思念的生活总会被幻相塞满。

现在谛视一些确定的终点，

　人事流逝，而我将证实

　在某处的一次相遇，爱和爱的相遇，

我恳求你的原谅，我的朋友；

我握住兄弟的手，用和从前一样真实的爱，

　如果爱不能新鲜如从前，

　即便我愿意，我也不能

将我为他而生的感情全部交付于你。

是什么使得青春岁月不同于其他的阶段？

　是最初的爱，最初的友谊，

是平等的两个人，
怀着纯洁之心结合。

我心依旧，禁不住悲悼，
　　在荒凉的地方独自跳动，
　　依旧记得他的拥抱，
但不再会朝向他的足迹，

我的心，尽管如孀妇一般，
　　无法在消失的爱中获致安宁，
　　却仍在时间中寻求
另一个与自己产生共鸣的人。

啊，请取走这份我带来的有缺陷的礼物，
　　要知道报春花依然可爱，
　　这一年晚些时候绽放的报春花，
不会和春天绽放的有什么区别。

八十六

阵雨后,芬芳、甜美的微风
　　升腾自傍晚湛蓝的雾霭中,
　　拂过灌木、花丛
和草地,缓慢地涤荡

这茫茫天宇,又转身向下
　　穿过所有缨穗带露的树木,
　　追逐流入海角的泛着涟漪的河水,
拂动我的眉梢,吹走

我面颊的潮热,感叹
　　这因你的友谊而哺育出的全新生命,
　　这微风遍及我全身,将怀疑和死亡,
这对不幸的兄弟赶走,令我畅想

可以和你长久地声气相投,这微风
　　在绯红的海面上沿着波光飘荡,
　　直至遇见遥远东方的晚星升起,
那儿有许多精灵低语着"安宁"。

八十七

我沿墙而过,在那可敬的
　　墙内,我曾身着长袍,
　　在大学城中随意漫游,
看见那些厅堂里的喧嚣;

也在学院教堂里再度听见
　　那巨大管风琴发出的轰鸣,
　　雷鸣般的音乐,滚动,摇晃
纹饰在窗格上的先知;

又再次捕捉到远处的叫喊,
　　在柳荫下,赛艇的桨划出
　　整齐的节拍,信步走过河边,
走过许多的桥,又再度走遍

那灰色的沙滩,恍若
　　一切重现,又有所不同,最后
　　走过长长的欧椴树道,我
去看他曾住过的房间。

另一个名字在门上:
　　我徘徊着,从里面传来
　　嘈杂的歌声与掌声,男孩们
敲着杯子,跺着地板;

我们也曾在这里辩论,一群
　　年轻友人,谈论思想和艺术,
　　以及劳工,变化中的市场,
和这片土地上的种种体制;

那时有人想要箭不虚发,
　　但离弦时已呈颓相,
　　还有人总是言不及义,
或偏于一隅,东一下西一下;

最后,他这精湛的射手,
　　将一击中的。我们乐于
　　听从他。谁,能不倾听
他专注的演说?那言辞轻快流动,

逐一而论,优雅、有力,
　　悦耳,不逾越律法的界限,

当抵达结论之际我们看见
他内在的神点亮他的脸庞,

似乎将那形体托起,光焰夺目
　　环绕着神圣的蔚蓝轨道,
　　在那非凡轻盈的眼睛之上,
那米开朗基罗的眉框。

八十八

野地里的鸟,你的啭鸣,清澈甜美,
    穿过蓓蕾初绽的树篱,召唤那乐园,
    哦,告诉我理智在何处交汇,
哦,告诉我激情在何处相遇,

又从何处散发,在暗下去的叶子中间,
    极端的情绪占据你的心,
    而在忧伤的正中央,
你的激情紧扣住秘密的欢乐:

而我——我的竖琴将奏起悲哀的序曲——
    我不能完全控制我的琴弦;
    那宇宙万物的荣耀
将在弦上一闪而过。

八十九

老榆树,在这平坦草地表面 *

 织满明暗交错的光影;

 还有你,身形如塔的无花果树,

从头到脚都披挂着绿叶;

不止一次地,当我们漫步至此,

 我的亚瑟发觉你们阴翳的美丽,

 那些市镇上的灰尘、喧嚣和紧张,

此刻都抖落在自由的空气中;

他对所见到的一切都抱有好奇,

 和我们完全打成一片;

 刚摆脱喧嚷的法庭 † 及其无趣的周边,

这些简单的娱乐令他满意。

他快乐地在树下休憩,

 浸没在芬芳的树荫里,

 啜饮清凉的空气,注视

那些闪动在炽热大地上的风光:

* 这首诗是回忆哈勒姆对诗人家乡的一次拜访。

† 哈勒姆曾是某个律师学院的成员。

哦,赶走成批烦忧的声音,
  在晨露中镰刀挥动,
  狂风绕着花园呼啸,
吹落了半数熟透的梨子!

哦至福,当同伴们凑成一个圆圈
  围向他,心灵和耳朵急切地想
  倾听他,当他在草地躺下,
读着托斯卡纳的诗人们[*]:

* 指但丁和彼特拉克,哈勒姆最喜爱的意大利诗人。

或是在灿烂的下午,
  一个客人或开心的姊妹,唱着歌,
  或者,她带来竖琴,向着明月
弹拨起一首歌谣:

在心情更放松的时候他还喜欢
  去群山之间漫游,
  用遥远森林中的野餐,
打破炎炎夏日的漫长;

在那里,我们的议题不断变化,
  交流喜欢和憎厌的书籍,

有时议论一下政事,
有时则穿行于有苏格拉底的梦境*; *喻指读柏拉图的著作。

但假如我赞扬城镇忙碌的生机,
    他就会针锋相对地抱怨它,
    抱怨在那社会工厂的碾磨下,
我们各自的棱角都会磨去,

他说,"城市会让每个人各自的独特生动,
    泯灭成千篇一律的模式与光鲜。"
    我们谈话:在我们下方溪水奔流,
酒瓶横卧在泥沼中,

抑或伴着向晚的波涛纳凉,
    在深红光晕的星星
    坠入西天之前,
我们从远处姗姗归来,

经过深及踝部的花丛,
    我们听到身后忍冬遮住
    在桶中咕咕作响的牛奶,
甜蜜的时光嗡嗡郁郁。

九十

[*] 暗指 Saadi 的 *Gu-listan* 这本书里的意思。

对于爱他所知甚少*,
 他从未啜饮过最接近天堂的
 未被污染的泉水,这最早在人群之中
抛洒苦涩种子的人;

他说,倘若曾在恸哭之声中紧闭的
 死者的眼睛,如今又睁开,
 他们重新开始的生命将只能
遭受妻儿的冷遇:

他说看起来的确不错,借着酒兴,
 妻儿会用亲切的泪水向死者承诺,
 反复谈论他们,盼望他们就在这里,
并把回忆渲染得神乎其神;

但他说,如果那些去世者当真归来,
 会看到他们的新娘挽着另一个人的手,
 而无情的子孙盘踞在他们的土地上,
将一天也不会向他们让步。

是的，即便他们的儿孙并非如此，
　　这位仍受爱戴的作者也将制造出
　　比死亡更为恶劣的混乱，且动摇
每个家庭和睦的基石。

啊亲爱的，但还是请你回到我身边，
　　不管岁月发生如何的改变，
　　我仍未发觉心里会有一丝杂念
在向我呼喊，在阻止我走向你。

九十一

当落叶松缀满玫红色的幼芽,
　　枝头画眉鸣出罕有的欢歌,
　　或是从光秃秃的灌木丛里
突然掠过三月海蓝色的翠鸟;

来,显现你的形体,我会辨识出
　　那个我大学时代最熟悉的灵魂,
　　未尽岁月的希望
在你额前,辽阔又清澈。

当夏日一点点成熟,变化了
　　五月的气息,伴随玫瑰的芬芳
　　在那环绕孤单田庄起伏着的
一千重麦浪之上;

来,但不要在无眠的长夜,
　　而在温暖日光下,
　　来,你死后形体的美丽,
像极好的,光中的光。

九十二

倘若任何幻象将你的面容
　　显现，我唯有把它视作
　　类似头脑病变般的徒劳，
是的，尽管它诉说，又求助于

一些偶然的场所，我们的命运曾被一起
　　抛掷在那里，抛掷在那些尘封的往昔，
　　我也许只能说，我听见的是记忆的风
在喃喃低语着过去。

是的，尽管这幻象诉说又窥见
　　一个未来岁月中的事实，
　　尽管那些月份，在近旁流转，
将证实那幽灵预告的真实，

这些幽灵的预告看起来可能并不出自你，
　　只是闯入我脑海的预感，
　　是诸如此类事件的折光，
像星辰在升起之前就时常浮现的光。

九十三

我确实将看不到你。但我怎敢说,
  当泥土合拢之际,
  不曾有灵成功地摆脱
那捆缚着令其远离故乡的柩绳?

没有什么可见的影子留下,
  但他,灵本身,会出现
  在所有感官神经探测不到之处;
灵向着灵,魂向着魂。

因此,从你与诸神同在的
  看不见的漫游中,在无须揣测的祝福中,
  从那历经复杂变幻的
十重天的深处,

请下降,触碰我,进入我;再请听见
  我那强烈到难以言表的愿望;
  在这形体无有知觉的地方,
我的魂可以感觉你就在身边。

九十四

需要怎样纯粹的心与健全的头脑,
    以及何等神圣强烈的情感,
    才能成为那个,可能与死者共度
一小时促席光阴的人。

你,或任何人,都将徒劳于
    从黄金岁月里呼唤出灵,
    除了,像他们一样,你也能说,
我的灵是和其他的灵一样安宁,

能拥有平静且公正的想象力,
    宛如晴空的澄澈记忆,
    以及像安宁的海一般的道德感,
他们才会时常造访你静默的胸膛:

而一旦你的心被喧嚣塞满,
    任怀疑守在天国的门前,
    那些灵就只会把耳朵贴在门上倾听,
听下界日常生活的震荡。

九十五

我们漫步在夜晚的草地,
  脚下的香草干爽怡人,
  天气温暖,月色如银
弥漫在夏日晴空里;

宁静得连小小烛光
  都不摇晃,蟋蟀也不鸣叫,
  只听得远处小溪的欢闹,
以及茶壶在炊架上咕咕作响:

在芬芳的天空下蝙蝠飞翔,
  夜蛾盘旋,抑或一闪一闪
  出没于暮色,它们有貂皮般的披风,
羊毛似的前胸,和珠状的眼睛;

这时我们开始唱古老的歌,
  歌声飘扬在山谷间,那里隐隐可见
  白色的母牛悠然而卧,而树木
把黑色的枝影投向原野。

但当那些其他的人一个接一个,
　　向我告辞,从夜色里退去,
　　屋子里的灯一盏接一盏
熄灭,剩下我独自一人,

一种饥饿感攫住我的心;我翻阅
　　那些来自死者的美好书简,
　　犹如翻阅一片片依然青翠的落叶,
我读到那惊鸿一现的欢乐年华:

沉默的话语奇异地打破
　　我的默读,奇异的是爱的哑默呼喊,
　　它把自己交给变化来检验,
并奇异地说出

那信念,那热力,并放胆去面对
　　那足以击退懦夫的怀疑,
　　且渴望穿越言辞的迷宫
去探寻内心最深处的密室。

就这样逐字又逐行,
　　那死者自过去触动我,

那鲜活的灵魂似乎最终
突然闪现在我的灵魂中,

而我的灵魂也缠绕在他的灵魂中,
　　在思想的最高天上急旋,
　　随后遭遇终极的存在,并把握
这个世界的深层脉动。

这永恒的音乐给时间
　　打着拍子,把生的偶然不定,
　　纳入死的和谐。我终于
从出神中醒转,伴随怀疑的困扰。

暧昧的文字!然而,那单纯物质性的
　　话语形式,是多么难以表达这体验,
　　即便殚精竭虑,也难以通过回忆
去抵达我所抵达之处:

如今,怀疑的薄暮散去,
　　露出曾经的山谷,那里隐隐可见
　　白色的母牛悠然而卧,而树木
把黑色的枝影投向原野:

随后这一切都卷入茫茫的曙色,
　　微弱的气息开始摇动
　　槭树宽大的叶子,
并将寂静的香气四处飘送,

这气息更为旺盛地聚集在上空,
　　晃动枝叶婆娑的榆树,并摇荡
　　重重紧裹的玫瑰,且将百合花
来回推动,并且说道,

"天亮了,天亮了,"随后就平息;
　　东方和西方,此刻没有一丝风,
　　它们的微光混融,像生和死的混融,
一同扩展成为无边无际的白昼。

九十六

> *这里的"你"是指一位女子,可能是作者后来的妻子 Emily Sellwood,也可能是作者的一位姐妹。

你*并不带任何轻蔑地说道,
 你这可爱的人,你淡蓝色的眼睛
 温柔地掠过溺水的飞蝇,
你告诉我,怀疑是撒旦之子。

我不知道:而我真的认识一个
 精通许多微妙问题的人,
 他先触到一架音调失衡的竖琴,
却曾努力要将之调校准确:

困惑于信念,却纯粹于行动,
 最终,他驯服了他的音乐。
 较之对教义的半信半疑,相信我,
在诚实的怀疑中会升腾更强烈的信。

他与他的怀疑战斗,并聚集力量,
 他不愿做出盲目的判断,
 面对心智的幽灵,
他降伏他们:因此他终于

发觉他自己一个更强悍的信念;
　　而上帝的权能与他相伴在
　　那制造了黑暗与光的夜,
祂不是单单栖身于光中,

也栖身在黑暗和阴云里,
　　如同在古老的西奈山顶上*,   * 参见《出埃及记》第19章,第33章。
　　尽管那号角吹得如此响亮,
以色列人仍蒙昧地做着金制的神像。

九十七

我的爱神已经在和岩石与树木交谈；
　　在雾中的山地上他发现
　　他自己无限且荣光奕奕的影子；
在一切所见之物中他看见自己。

一段婚姻生活的两个侣伴——
　　我看着他们，想到你
　　正处于广袤与神秘之中，
而我的灵之于你如同妻子之于丈夫。

这样的两个人——他们的眼睛里只有对方
　　他们旧日的心灵一起跳动，
　　他们的相聚能令寒冬变成盛夏，
他们每一次分离都宛如死别。

他们的爱从不消散；
　　她绝不可能忘记那些
　　他发誓会一直爱她的日子，
无论那些无信仰的人们说些什么。

她独自生活,他隔岸而坐,
　　他仍然爱她,她将不会哭泣,
　　尽管因为专注于黑暗和深渊的事宜,
他看起来怠慢了她单纯的心。

他穿过心智的迷宫,
　　阅读群星的秘密,
　　他看起来如此近又如此远,
他看起来如此冷酷:她想他是仁慈的。

她保留着从前岁月的礼物
　　一朵枯萎的紫罗兰就令她欢欣
　　她不认识他的伟大究竟为何,
因此,尽管如此,她更爱他了。

她弹着音乐,对他唱着
　　早年的信念和签订的誓约;
　　她仅仅知道家屋的事情,
而他,他知道万事万物。

她的信念已定,不能动摇,
　　她模糊地感觉他的伟大与智慧,

她用忠贞的眼睛凝思他,
"我不能理解:我爱。"

九十八

你 * 离开我们：你将看见莱茵河，
  看见河水两岸的美丽山坡，
  我和他曾一起顺河而下；
你将沿着夏日里连绵起伏的麦浪与葡萄园

去那个他咽下最后一口气的地方，
  那个城市。而那城市所有的荣光
  似乎也难比死神所看到的
忘川上的一缕磷火。

让伟大的多瑙河继续围绕群岛
  优美起伏，这与我无关：
  我已无法看见，我将不会看见，
维也纳；我只是梦见那里，

梦见三重的黑暗，恶魔出没于
  新生与新婚，朋友们
  不断被分开，年迈的父亲
不断在子女坟墓前屈身，千种欲望

* 这里的"你"，可能指丁尼生的兄弟查尔斯，他在 1836 年去莱茵河一带蜜月旅行，而丁尼生和哈勒姆在 1832 年也有过一次类似的旅行。查尔斯这次旅程的目的地是维也纳，恰好是哈勒姆去世的地方。

紧跟在人的身后咆哮,沿着
　　每一个寒冷的炉边捕猎,
　　而悲哀把她的影子投向列王的火焰:
而我自己却听见他说,

没有任何一个大都市有着
　　如此恢弘庄严的
　　来回流动的车河,流过
被如此茂密树荫覆盖的

乐园和郊区;他告诉我,
　　在哪儿都没有在这里开心,
　　当所有人纵情于灯火,放声
歌唱和玩乐,在摊位前和帐篷里,

在帝国的宫廷,或开阔的原野;
　　他们跳着环形的轮舞,燃放焰火,
　　这焰火在天空爆裂成深红色碎片
抑或化作一阵翠雨落下。

九十九

你就这样升起，黯淡的黎明*，再一次   * 这一天是哈勒姆
   伴着群鸟纷飞的喧闹，   的逝世两周年，
   伴着牛群低沉的呼叫，   9月15日。参看
这一天，我失去人类之花的这一天；   第72首。

透过朦胧的霞光你颤动
   在远处湍急暴涨的溪水上，
   这溪水流过诉说往事的草地，
流过死者心爱的树林；

你在枝叶扶疏的屋檐下
   轻哼一首对未来不管不顾的歌，
   而秋天正将火焰的手指
扫过一处又一处的树叶；

你用温馨的气息唤醒
   和悦大地上的众生，
   教他们记起婚礼，或出生的时节，
也让无数的人记起死。

哦,无论他们身在何处,

　　在地球昏沉迟滞的两极之间,

　　今天他们都算是我的亲人;

他们不认识我,却和我一同哀悼。

一〇〇 *

我爬上那座山：从这端到那头
  山下的风景从眼前一一掠过，
  我发现无处不在诉说
一些亲切回忆，关于我的朋友；

不止是寂寞的羊栏，灰旧的田庄，
  低处的沼泽和低语的芦苇，
  草地之间的简单梯磴，
以及多风的荒原之上的牧场；

不止是古老的布满火山灰与山楂的丘陵，
  那儿听见红雀在近旁啁啾；
  不止是沿着小山凿出的沟渠
萦绕着寒鸦的争鸣；

不止是流水自岩石中奏出银铃；
  也不止是乡村的小溪突然转向
  忽左忽右蜿蜒穿过草场，
滋养这里的人群。

* 这首诗，及下面几首，都涉及丁尼生全家自萨默斯比老家筹划搬迁至北伦敦艾坪森林地区的事。

而是它们中的每一样都愉悦了我们，
　　都唤起某个更温柔的日子，
　　然后丢下这一切，这一切消失于暮色，
他好像在我面前又死去了一次。

一〇一

不被看见的，深院里的树枝仍将摇动，
    柔弱的花朵将盛开又纷纷落下，
    不被爱上的，那棵山毛榉将渐次变成褐色，
而这棵枫树也将燃尽它自身；

不被爱上的，向日葵，明媚闪烁，
    围绕它种籽的花盘射出火苗，
    许多玫瑰康乃馨把夏日的芳香
播撒入嗡嗡作响的空气中；

不被爱上的，小溪仍蜿蜒越过众多沙洲
    再潺潺流向平原，
    无论是正午，还是
小熊星座围绕北极星转动的夜晚；

不被在意的，一轮明月笼住多风的树林，
    又涌进苍鹭和秧鸡的眠处，
    又或者如银色的利箭
射入每一道河湾；

直到从这庭院和郊野
  传来某种新的关系,
  而年复一年,陌生人的孩子
也熟悉了这片风光;

就像劳作者年复一年耕耘
  他们熟悉的土地,整饬林地;
  年复一年,我们的记忆
也将从这一带山陵间褪去。

一〇二

我们离开深爱的土地,
  那儿我们初次看见苍穹;
  那听见过我们最初哭喊的屋宇
将庇护另一户陌生人家。

我们走了,但在离开家园以前,
  当我沿着花园小径独行,
  两颗不同的爱的心灵
却开始争夺起爱的支配权。

一个低语:"这是你童年时
  晨祷放歌之处,你曾在这儿听见
  鸟儿轻声低吟的爱的言语
在故乡垂满花朵的榛树林中。"

另一个回答:"是的,但这儿更是
  你成年后与你失去的友人
  林荫下四处漫游之所,
是这样才使得它们愈发亲切。"

这两个声音争执不下,
　　每一个都提出他独特的断言,
　　一场徒劳的比赛中两个可怜的对手
彼此都不屈服。

我转身离去：我拖动双脚
　　离开这宜人的田野和庄园；
　　那两个对手彼此挽着臂膀
融合成一个遗憾的背影。

一〇三

在那个最后的夜晚,在我们离开
　　从被哺育的门中走出之前,
　　我梦见死者的幻象,
晨曦消散之后仍使我满足。

我以为我曾居住在一座宫殿,
　　为少女们所环绕:那从群山深处
　　看不见的峰顶蜿蜒而下的小溪
汇成河流,沿着殿墙外流淌。

宫殿洋溢着竖琴和赞美诗的声音,
　　她们歌唱的是智慧、善
　　以及仁慈。在中央我看见
一座蒙着面纱的雕像,她们对着他歌唱;

他尽管蒙着面纱,仍为我所熟知,
　　那是我爱过并将永远爱着的
　　他的形体:随后飞进一只鸽子
从永恒的海上带来一声召唤:

我必须离去的消息令她们哭泣悲叹，
　　但随后，她们就引领我
　　走向一只停泊在
低处河湾中的小舟；

驶过许多平坦的草地，
　　驶过投下阴影的夹岸峭壁，
　　我们蜿蜒滑行在
鸢尾花和金色芦苇的阵列下；

海岸线变得越来越广阔，
　　在更宏大的领域中席卷起浪花，
　　少女们集聚起她们的力量、优雅
和风度，比以往更高贵；

而我自己，独自坐着
　　观看她们，一点点变得强健；
　　我感觉亚衲金人的肌肉，
一个泰坦心脏的搏动；

她们将依次歌唱，歌唱战争的消失，
　　颂扬那个属于未来的

伟大族群的历史,
又诉说星辰是怎样形成;

直到蜿蜒前行的潮汐
 泛起泡沫,我们启航
 去往永恒的深处,那里我们看见
一艘巨轮升起闪亮的船舷。

我们爱的那个人在甲板上,
 身躯长大了三倍,他屈身
 欢迎我们。我走上甲板
和他沉默相拥:

随即那些少女不约而同地
 悲恸她们的命运;我辜负了她们:
 "我们在这儿侍奉你这么久,"她们说,
"而你此后就要离开我们吗?"

我是如此出神,她们不能从我的嘴中
 赢取一个回答,但他回复道:
 "你们也一同进来
和我们在一起":她们于是进来。*

* 少女们象征此世和早年生活的希望与力量。丁尼生想表明,人们不该为了死后生活(来世)而抛弃此世给予自己的那些美好,来世和此世不是对立的,后者是前者的准备,"她们于是进来"。

此刻风开始吹,
　　在船板和桅索之间呼啸,
　　我们行进,向着远处地平线上
低垂的、沐浴在天堂光辉中的红云。

一〇四

基督的诞辰临近了*;

　　月亮藏起,夜晚寂静,

　　山脚下被裹入薄雾的小教堂

钟声正敲响。

那下方一阵孤单的钟声,

　　在这个休憩时刻

　　唤起一阵轻微的抱怨,

这不是我所熟知的钟声。

它们听起来像陌生人的低语,

　　在一块毫无记忆存留的土地,

　　也没有地标可联想起往日,

这只是一块未被圣化的新区。

* 这具体是指1837年圣诞,诗人的家庭在这一年的五月从林肯郡萨默斯比搬家到了埃赛克斯郡的艾坪森林附近,靠近伦敦。这首诗是诗集中第三次出现圣诞节,是在一个新的陌生地方迎接新的圣诞节。

一〇五

今夜,让我们不再去采摘
　　月桂的枝条,也留下这冬青屹立:
　　我们生活在陌生人的土地,
我们的平安夜奇异地降临。

我们父亲的骨灰被独自留在原处,
　　沉寂在另外一些雪的下面:
　　那儿忍冬在适当时候随风飘动,
紫罗兰开放,但我们已离去。

不必再怀着难以控制的悲伤
　　去勉强做那些猜面具的游戏和表演,
　　因为环境的变化,就像时间的生长,
已教人摆脱那些陈旧习俗的束缚。

让忧愁投下一些细碎的阴影,
　　借此我们的生命才得以证明,
　　让这个我爱的夜晚分出少许空闲,
可以用于认真地怀想过去。

但不要再让脚步叩击地板，
　　也不作觥筹交错的礼仪；
　　既然魂魄已不在此地，
谁又会把古老的形式循沿？

不要唱歌，游戏，也不要宴会，
　　不要弹奏竖琴，不要吹响长笛，
　　不要舞蹈，不要星光，
除了那沿着远处森林冉冉升起的

点亮明晰东方的晨星。
　　夏日长久地睡在种子里；
　　生命按季节有序地转动，
跃向那充满善的闭合的环。

一〇六

敲响吧,狂暴的钟声,向着狂野天空,
　　向着流云,向着霜寒的光:
　　这一年就将逝去,在这个夜晚;
敲响吧,狂暴的钟声,让它消失。

敲走旧日,敲来新岁,
　　敲吧,欢乐的钟声,踏雪而来:
　　这一年就要结束,让它结束;
敲走错误,敲来真实。

敲走削弱心智的哀痛,
　　为了那些我们无法再见的一切;
　　敲走贫富之间的长久争执,
敲来对于全体人类的匡正。

敲走一种渐趋濒死的事业,
　　以及老旧的党派相争的政体,
　　敲来更为高尚的生活方式,
伴随更优美的风尚,更纯粹的法律。

敲走匮乏，焦虑和罪恶，
　　以及旧时代种种冷酷与不义；
　　敲响吧，敲走我悲哀的韵词，
但要敲来更为完整的歌手。

敲走基于地位和血统的虚荣，
　　以及市井小民的流言与刁难；
　　敲来对于真理和正义的爱，
以及对于善的普遍共同的爱。

敲走旧有的种种恶疾与弊病；
　　敲走对于金钱一意孤行的贪欲；
　　敲走往昔成千上万次的战争，
敲来人间的千年和平。

敲来英勇和自由的人类，
　　更为宽阔的心灵，和更为亲切的手；
　　敲走大地上的黑暗，
敲来那就要降临的基督。

一〇七

这一天是他出生的日子,
　　苦涩的白昼,早早沉没在
　　雾气弥漫的霜紫色海岸之外,
只留下孤独的夜晚。

时令不允许鲜花或绿叶
　　装点这宴会。狂风呼啸着
　　从东北方向吹来,而冰霜
在锋利的屋檐边凝结成匕首,

所有的灌木与荆棘都惊耸地朝向
　　远处清冷的新月,仿佛她被吊在
　　林梢,在吱嘎作响的树干
和冻得发硬的枝桠上方。

同时,大团的流云掠过,
　　弄暗了翻滚着击打堤岸的
　　海水。但且把酒取来,
排好餐桌,倒满酒杯;

再加点粗大的木块,将它们平放,
　　燃起不易熄灭的火;
　　且高兴起来,闲聊和讨论
各种事情,好像他就在身边;

我们纪念这一天。以节日的欢呼,
　　以书籍和音乐,无论他化作什么,
　　我们当然要为他干杯,
并唱那些他喜爱听见的歌。

一〇八

我不会茕茕孑立于众人之外,
  并且,为避免僵硬成石头,
  我不会独自啃噬自己的心,
不会在风中徒自叹息:

贫瘠的信仰与茫然的渴求
  又有何益?尽管伴随着强力
  要去攀登天堂最高的顶端,
或纵身跃入死的深渊。

在最高处我发现了什么,
  除了呢喃着诗篇的自我的幽灵?
  而在死渊里游弋的
不过是一张人类之脸的倒影。

我宁可在人类的天空之下
  摘取那可能属于悲恸的果实,
  而无论何种智慧随你沉睡,
据说悲恸仍能使我们明智。

一〇九

丰富的心灵,流溢在闲谈中,
　　源自永不枯竭的涓滴日常;
　　批评家独具只眼的清明,
看清所有缪斯漫步的道路; *

*哈勒姆死前已出版过一些非常成熟的批评文论。

六翼天使的智慧与伟力
　　理解并瓦解人的怀疑;
　　充满激情的推理,让听众
难以跟上这燃烧般的思路;

崇高的天性爱慕善,
　　但没有感染一丝苦行的阴郁;
　　在热血沸腾的青春年华
纯洁的激情如雪般盛开;

一种对于自由的独特感受与热爱,
　　热爱端坐在英格兰庄严王座上的
　　自由,它并非学童的狂热,
并非凯尔特人盲目的疯狂;

男性气概又融合了女性的优雅,
　　就连孩子们都会主动地
　　把手信任地放在你手中,
你的面容使他们感到安心;

所有这些已发生的,还有你,
　　都曾是我所亲见:如果它们全然徒劳,
　　如果你的智慧不能使我明智,
我会比一切未亡人都羞愧。

一一〇

你的交谈欣然引领我们这些
  或年轻或衰老的人:
  虚弱的灵魂,诸多恐惧出没之所,
却在你的目光中忘记他的软弱。

内心忠实的人依靠你,
  骄傲的人渐渐解除他的骄傲,
  在你身边,狡猾者也不再会
鼓动他如簧的巧舌。

当你在身边,严厉的人也变得温和,
  轻浮的人虚心学习
  并聆听你,愚顽厚颜者
也被软化,他自己不知道为什么;

而我,你最亲近的,站在一边,
  感觉你的胜利就如同我的,
  并无比热爱这属于你的,
优雅的机敏,基督徒的技艺;

我并不拥有这些美妙与技艺,
　我只拥有永不疲倦的爱,
　以及一种源自爱的
鼓励我效仿你的朦胧热望。

一二一

精神上的自由民,沿着浩荡的行列
　　向上或向下,穿过所有等级的人,
　　走向手握权杖宝珠的那个人,
那王者的血统,不羁的心;

精神上的自由民,无论他怎样
　　用各种形式来避免追逐时尚,
　　他活力四射的天性依旧会掀开
社交季节里重重镀金的面罩:

因为谁能够始终驾驭舞台?唯有他,
　　在这方面留给我们无数的回忆
　　他举手投足间的风采,
完全是一个标准的绅士,

他竭尽所能,使得贵族风范
　　就像从高贵心智中
　　自然生长出来的鲜花
彰显在社交季的每一处场所;

在他的眼神中从未有过
 褊狭或怨恨,也没有什么
 一闪而过的恶念,
上帝与自然在他的目光中相遇;

因此,他从容向前,从不辱没
 绅士这辉煌古老的名称,
 这名称曾遭欺世盗名者的诽谤,
也曾被卑鄙的事所玷污。

一一二

高等智慧看轻了我的智慧,
　　因为我, 用温和的眼睛凝视
　　那神采奕奕的欠缺,
无视那些相对狭隘的完美。

唯有你, 充满我全部爱的
　　空间的你, 是我为什么
　　淡漠相看那些完美灵魂的原因,
他们虽掌握命运, 却仍小于你。

你已成为什么? 一些新奇的力量
　　一经触动就生生不息,
　　在对你时时刻刻的观看中,
永远都存在新的可能,

众多元素秩序井然地产生,
　　从暴风雨中生出平静的土地,
　　在追随思想而生的潮汐中
整个世界随之波动, 摇摆。

一一三

有人认为悲哀使我们明智,
　然而多少智慧随你沉睡,
　这智慧不仅曾引领我,
而且也服务于那些或会到来的时局;

既然我如此了解你,又怎会怀疑你
　心智的敏锐,伴随力量与才干
　去奋斗,去改变,去完成——
我从不怀疑你可能会成为的样子:

一种献身公众行动的生活,
　一个传达最高使命的灵魂,
　一个议会中强有力的声音,
一根风暴中坚定的柱石,

在时机成熟的时候,
　一旦大众获得许可的勇气聚集起力量,
　你会成为那撬动地球的杠杆,
并推动这个国家进入另一条轨道,

伴随来来去去的成千种震动,
　　伴随斗争,伴随活力,
　　伴随倾覆,伴随哭喊
以及往复不息的波涌。

一一四

谁不喜爱知识?谁会抱怨
　　她的美?愿她使人类
　　迈入兴旺。谁会限定
知识的疆域?让她所向披靡。

但欲火熊熊燃烧在她额头:
　　她纵容着自己一往无前,
　　热衷攫取未来的机遇,
让一切屈从于自己的渴望。

然而如同既不成熟又虚荣的小孩子——
　　她不能抵挡死亡的恐惧。
　　她是什么?割舍了爱和真理,
她不过是某个狂野的帕拉斯*,从神灵的

头颅中跃出。急切地摧毁着
　　她在权力竞赛中的障碍。
　　须让她知晓她的位置,
她是次级,而非首席。

> * 即智慧女神雅典娜,从宙斯的头颅中生出。

倘若一切并非空幻，一只更高的手
  定会使她温顺，引导
  她的步伐，让她随智慧
并肩移动，像个更年轻的孩子：

因她只拥有世俗的心智，
  而灵魂的圣化才带来智慧。
  哦，朋友，你如此过早地
抵达智慧的目标，将我抛在身后，

我愿这伟大的尘世能如你一样，
  不断生长，不单单在力量和知识上
  生长，而是能够经年累月地
生长，在信与爱中。

一一五

如今最后长条的积雪已消融,
  如今每一道纷乱的树篱都发芽
  开出花的广场,密密麻麻
挨着梣树的根,紫罗兰绽放。

如今林地间的鸣响嘹亮悠长,
  远处蒙上一层可爱的色泽,
  在鲜艳蓝天尽处隐没的
云雀,留下一首看不见的歌。

如今光影闪烁在草地牧场,
  沿着溪谷,羊群更显得洁白,
  无论在蜿蜒的河流还是遥远的海上,
每一张白帆都如牛乳一般;

如今那儿海鸥尖叫,或俯身跃过
  远处绿色的波光,幸福的候鸟
  振翅飞往另一片天空,
去筑巢和繁衍;尽其可能地生活

从一处到另一处；在我心里
　　春天也醒来；我的遗憾
　　就变成一束四月的紫罗兰，
萌芽，开花，一如别的事物。

一一六

那么，尤为强烈地在甜美四月里萌生的
　　就只是这种对于冬日蛰伏时光的遗憾么？
　　就是要怀抱这样的遗憾来迎接新的一年，
让春天染上哀愁，又被春天所安慰么？

并不尽然：那些歌，虫鸣迭荡的空气，
　　破土而出的生命重新适应着
　　透过感官去呼喊，去信任
那些使世界如此美丽的事物。

并非只有遗憾：那张面容将闪耀
　　在我之上，当我独自沉思；
　　而那我曾了解的，亲切的声音，
仍对我说着一些和我有关的事情：

而一想起那些曾和逝者相守的幸福时日，
　　我心底的悲哀也渐渐减轻；
　　如今我渴望的，与其说是消逝的友谊，
毋宁说是某些即将实现的强力结合。

一一七

哦光阴,你的作用就是这样
　　引领我走出自身的局限,
　　并短暂脱离他的拥抱,
为着属于死后福祉的更完满的收获:

真希望随距离而生的渴望
　　可以加深两人亲昵时的甜蜜;
　　这样等到我们再次相见时,
会自然累积出难以估量的欢乐,

为着每颗滴落的沙粒,
　　每段溜走的阴影,
　　每一对齿轮的啮合, *
以及日月星辰的一次次流转。

*这三行分别指沙漏、日晷和时钟。

一一八

请审思时间的一切工作,
  这在青春中劳作的巨人,
  不要把人类爱和真理的梦想,
视作终有一死的物种的尘灰;

而是要相信,那些我们称之为死者的
  是在一种更丰富的时日中呼吸,
  为着更高贵的目标。他们[*]说,
我们脚下那坚实的土地

起源于大块流荡的噫气,
  长成似乎随机的形状,
  风暴循环肆虐于地表,
直至最终出现了人;

他兴盛,繁衍,从一处到另一处,
  预报着一个更高物种的到来,
  预言他自身,将处于更高的位置,
如果它能在自己身上重现

* 他们,指当时提出星云假说或地质灾变论的一批科学家,如居维叶,拉普拉斯等。

这时间的劳作,不断地拓展自我;
　　抑或,戴上象征苦难的荆冠,
　　满怀荣耀,奋力向前,
表明生命并非无用的废矿,

而是铁石,掘自阴暗的地心,
　　被强烈的恐惧灼烧至滚烫,
　　再淬入嘶嘶作响的泪水之池,
并经受命运之锤的重击,

以便成形、可用。起身超越
　　那踉跄的羊人*,和感官的享受,　　　＊指性欲。
　　向上,从兽性中摆脱,
弃绝愚蠢与残暴的形骸。

一一九

> 大门[*]，我心曾经激烈跳动的
> 　　地方，我再一次前来，
> 　　却不再哭泣；整个城市熟睡；
> 我在街上嗅到草场的气息；
>
> 我听见一声鸟鸣；我看见
> 　　在两排久久沉默的黑暗门楣之间
> 　　属于最初黎明的一道浅蓝，
> 就想起最初的日子还有你，
>
> 就祝福你，为你的双唇是温柔的，
> 　　为你饱含友爱的双眼的明亮；
> 　　还来不及发出一声叹息
> 我就被你的双手所环抱。

[*] 参见第7首。

一二〇

我相信我没有虚度生命:
　　我以为我们并非只有大脑,
　　一种电磁的赝品; 并非徒然,
像保罗与野兽战斗, 我与死神战斗;

并非只是机巧铸成肉体的黏土:
　　就让科学证明我们是这样吧,
　　然而科学之于人类有何用处?
至少对我而言有何用处? 我不会甘于这样。

让他, 未来世代出现的
　　更高的智者, 摆脱幼年的形状
　　举止如更高级的猿类吧,
但我生来就要成为别的事物。

一二一

悲伤的黄昏星越过落日
  准备停当,你,随他奔赴死亡,
  你看着一切事物越来越
模糊,荣耀的时刻:

牛儿卸下身上的轭套,
  小舟渐渐靠近港湾,
  生命的灵光已暗淡,
你留神倾听正在关闭的门。

明亮的晨星,因夜色愈发鲜艳,
  通过你,尘世又开启劳作的声音,
  还有早起的鸟儿也在歌唱,
在你身后,更大的光*降临:

贩鱼船沿河而行,
  岸边有呼唤它的声音,
  你听着村庄里铁锤的叮当,
看牛队艰难地向前移动。

---

* 据《创世记》1:16:And God made two great lights; the greater light to rule the day, and the lesser light to rule the night: he made the stars also."更大的光"指白昼。

亲爱的昏星-晨星,双重的名字
　为同一个事物,那最初的,也是最后的,
　你,如我的此刻与过去,
你的位置在改变,你始终如一。

一二二

哦，最亲爱的，你会随我一起么，
　　当我从悲伤中振作起来，
　　渴望冲破层叠的幽暗，
让不朽的天国再次显现，

再次感觉，在平静的敬畏中，
　　强力的想象转动着
　　我灵魂四周群星闪烁的天宇，
她所有的运动都与律法合辙；

倘若你和我在一起，那墓穴未曾
　　将我们分离，此刻我们同在，
　　你的灵进入我四肢百骸，
直到我的血，彻底翻腾，

伴随更具活力的呼吸加速奔流，
　　像一个轻率的孩童，
　　随着早年欢乐的闪现，
我摆脱生与死的思虑；

所有幻想的微风拂过,
　每一颗露珠绘出一道彩虹,
　不可思议的闪电在深处耀动,
每种思想迸发出玫瑰一朵。

一二三

深渊翻滚之处,曾长满树木,
  大地,你已目睹多少改变!
  在那长街喧嚷的地方,
曾拥有海中央的沉静。

山陵是幻影,从一种形体
  流向另一种,无物可以驻留;
  它们雾一般消散,那坚实的土地,
像云,它们形成稍纵即逝的自我。

但我将存在于我的精神之中,
  梦着我的梦,引以为真;
  尽管我的唇也许低语着离辞,
我无法设想告别的事实。

一二四

那我们胆敢向之祈求赐福的；
　　我们至爱的信仰；我们可怕的怀疑；
　　他，他们，一，一切，在内，在外；
那我们设想的、黑暗中的权能；

在尘世或星辰间，在鹰翅下，
　　或昆虫的眼中，我都不能找到他，
　　人们在那些问题前虚耗力气，
我们已织出的只是琐碎的蛛网：

要是信仰已沉沉睡去，
　　我就会听见怀疑主义的叫喊，
　　听见在无神论的深渊中
一个不定形的海岸不断坍塌的声音；

然而胸口的温暖终将融化
　　冻结的理性中最冷漠的部分，
　　然后，心就像一个愤怒的男人，
站起来回答道"我已察觉"。

不，心更像一个陷入怀疑和恐惧的孩子：

  不过那盲目的叫喊恰使我清醒；

  而我曾经就像一个哭泣的孩子，

哭泣着，却知道他的父就在一旁；

如今不朽的灵魂再次目睹

  目睹人所不能理解的一切；

  瞧，那穿越自然、从黑暗中

伸出的双手，正在把人类塑造。

一二五

无论我的言辞或诗篇讲述了什么,
  我的竖琴总会奏出一些苦涩的音符,
  是的,虽然这样看起来,
在言语上总是有一些矛盾,

然而我从未丧失过希望;
  一直努力睁开日益黯淡的眼睛;
  或者,这矛盾只是爱神在播弄仁慈的谎言,
因为在真理的问题上他应当是坚定的:

如果那诗篇充满忧虑的关切,
  那是爱神在吐露诗的精魂;
  如果那言辞甜美而有力,
那是爱神烙上了高贵的印记;

请与我同在,直至我启航
  去寻找你,在神秘之渊,
  而那感官神经的电流,虽保持
一千次脉冲的舞蹈,却仍随躯体消逝。

一二六

爱神从来就是我的主人和国王,
　　在他面前,我注意听取
　　信使时时刻刻带来的
有关我朋友的音讯。

爱神从来就是我的国王与主人,
　　将来也是,尽管我至今仍深陷于
　　他在地上的廷堂,
在他忠诚卫士的包围中入睡,

并且时不时地能听到
　　某个走来走去的哨兵,
　　在深夜还冲着茫茫太空
私语,说一切安好。

一二七

而一切安好,尽管信仰脱离了
 它旧日的形体,在恐惧的夜;
 但有一个更深沉的声音穿过风暴,
听到的人会接受这风暴的咆哮,

这声音宣告一个普世的真理和正义
 将流传开来,尽管在接二连三的反复中 *
 塞纳河上红色的暴民
最终竟用死尸筑起街垒。

* 指发生在1789年、1830年和1848年的三次法国革命。

尽管对于王者和衣衫褴褛的民众,
 情况确实都有些糟糕:
 他们发抖,如勉强支撑着的峭壁;
冰的尖顶坍塌,

融化,上涨,咆哮成大水;
 堡垒自高处崩塌,
 残忍的大地在天空下发亮,
伟大的永世在血中沉没,

被地狱烈火环绕；
　　然而你，亲爱的精灵，幸福之星，
　　从远处俯瞰这骚动，
微笑，知道一切安好。

一二八

升腾自强力羽翼上的爱,
  不会在死亡面前瘫痪,
  它是残存信仰的盟友
这信仰目睹人类向上的征程。

毫无疑问,奔腾向前的时间洪流
  仍将不断生成巨大的漩涡,
  飞扬一时的族群会衰退;
然而,你们善的神秘,

随希望和恐惧飞翔的野蛮时日,
  倘若你们所有不得不完成的,
  不过是新瓶装旧酒的工作;
倘若你们在此地全部的任务

就是将无用的刀剑出鞘入鞘,
  是用华丽的谎言愚弄民众,
  是把一种教义割裂成宗派与喧嚷,
是扭曲词与物的关系,

就是抛售一种专横的力量,
    是把学子束缚在课桌前,
    是粉饰过时的贫瘠,
且用牧草装点封建时代的塔楼;

那么,我何必要费心纠缠于此呢。
    某种程度上我所看见的,
    如同在一些艺术作品中所发生的,
是一切辛劳都朝向一个终点。

一二九

亲爱的友人，久远的，我已丧失的渴望，
　如此远，又如此近，在休戚之间，
　哦当我越察觉低劣与高贵的差异，
我就会更加地爱你。

已知的和未知的；人，和神；
　甜美的人类之手，人类的双唇和眼睛；
　亲爱的天国的友人，不会死去的友人，
我的，我的，永远，永远属于我；

陌生的友人，过去，现在，以及未来，
　在愈黑暗的领悟中爱得愈深；
　瞧，我梦着一个善的梦，
把整个世界和你融为一体。

一三〇

你的声音在滚动的风里;
 我听见你,在流逝的水里;
 你站在初升的太阳中,
在落日中的你如此美丽。

如今你是什么?我难以猜测;
 尽管我似乎在星辰和花朵中
 感受到你不断向外扩展的力,
这并不能削弱我对你的爱:

我的爱将往昔之爱尽数吸纳;
 如今又成为更阔大的深情;
 尽管你已同上帝和自然融为一体,
我却似乎越来越爱你。

你已远去,又永在我身旁;
 我仍然拥有你,并为此喜悦;
 我成熟,在你声音的怀抱里;
即使我死去,也不再会失去你。

一三一

当所有表象都遭受重创之际,
  那必能经受住考验的自由意志,
  请自灵磐石中升起,
请流过我们的功绩,使之纯粹,

我们的声音会自尘灰中升起,
  径直抵达倾听一切的袖,
  一声哭喊越过那些被迫臣服的岁月,
抵达那个伴随我们的人,而我们会相信,

凭着出自克己的信仰去相信真理,
  这真理是无法证明的,
  直到我们靠近我们爱过的故友,
靠近我们所有人的源泉,那灵魂中的灵魂。

终曲 [*]

[*] 这是一首婚典颂诗,为了祝贺诗人的小八岁的妹妹塞西莉亚与他的朋友、希腊文教授埃德蒙·勒欣顿成婚。这场婚礼是在1842年10月举行的,距离哈勒姆的死已经九年。诗人曾经在第85首诗中提到过勒欣顿。
[†] 指勒欣顿。
[‡] 指哈勒姆。
[§] 这一段意指哈勒姆与诗人另一个妹妹艾米莉的订婚。"黑色的一天"指哈勒姆突然病故的那一天。

真实,可靠,如此美好且持久,
　你[†]不需要一首婚姻的短诗;
　因为今天是你的结婚日,
音乐便胜过任何的诗歌。

这样巨大的幸福我已久违,上一次
　还是他[‡]告诉我,爱上了我们家里的
　一个姊妹;同样久违的是这美妙的
婚典,自那黑色的一天降临以来;[§]

自那之后尽管我已数过
　三个三年的日子:日子去了又来,
　血液更新,形体变化,
然而爱却有增无减;

不再焦虑于如何在死亡之歌里
　铭记死者的憾意,
　而是像一座实心的雕像
铸造出巨大的平静。

憾意消亡，爱却更深，

  深过那些已成过去的夏天，

  因我自己伴随这些也在成长，

向着某种比先前更好的样子；

这让我写下了一些歌，

  像从更为虚弱的岁月里逃逸出的回声，

  像尚未完成却已空洞喧嚷的韵脚，

阳光与阴影随性的游戏。

但她在哪儿？这新婚之花，

  在正午前必将成为一个妻子，

  她走进来，像伊甸园的月亮一样

照耀着她的婚房：

她把祝福的眼神投向我，

  随即再投向你；他们见到你的容颜，

  熠熠生辉，像星辰闪烁

在天堂的手掌间。

当她还是含苞欲放的生命，

  他* 就曾预言过这成熟的玫瑰。

* 指哈勒姆当年来丁尼生家中拜访时曾预言这位小妹妹以后的美。

她为你长成,还在为你继续生长,
　　永远,美与善的结合。

而你与她般配;既充满力量;
　　又温和文雅;开明,卓越,
　　坚定;满腹学问
又信手拈来犹如拈花。

但现在出发吧:正午已临近,
　　而我必须交出这位新娘*;
　　她一点都不害怕,抑或因为身旁是你
而身后是我,她不会害怕。

> *因为丁尼生的父亲早逝,所以婚礼上由作为兄长的丁尼生来负责把新娘交给新郎。

对于曾拉着她在我膝边雀跃的我,
　　曾注视她躺在保姆怀中的我,
　　曾时刻保护她免受伤害的我
终于,必须要将她交付于你;

现在,她在等待成为一个妻子,
　　她的足,我亲爱的,踏在死者的上方,
　　他们沉思的碑牌环绕在她头顶†,
而生命中最生动的言辞

> †意指她站在埋有地下墓穴的教堂中,而死者的纪念碑牌在四周的墙上。

在她耳边回荡。钟声响起,
　"你愿意吗",答复之后再一次
　被问及,"你愿意吗",如此交换,
她甜美的"我愿意",使你们合一。

现在请签上你们的名字*,它们　　　　　* 指在教堂记事
　将在另一个欢快的早晨,被另一些　　　录上签名。
　尚未出生的孩子们读到,
那名字已署好,而在空中

叮当作响的钟声也在把欢乐
　告知给每一丝漫游的微风;
　钟楼封闭的墙体震动,树梢上
那些落叶也在钟声中摇落。

哦幸福的时辰,更为幸福的时辰
　在等待着他们。许多欢快的面孔
　向他们致意——那是大厅里的少女们,
她们把鲜花洒向门廊中的我们。

哦幸福的时辰,请看着新娘
　与他偕行,我把她的手交付给他。

他们离开门廊，又穿过

此刻正洒满阳光的墓地。

今天，这墓地对我而言也是明朗的，

  对他们而言生命之光更为闪亮，

  谁留下分享仪式后的圣餐，

谁今夜要在海边憩息。*

> *这两行指婚礼仪式之后的圣餐和蜜月旅程。

让我衷心祝愿

  一个更灿烂明媚的白昼；

  我疲惫的记忆不会拒绝

法国香槟绚烂的气泡。

人们围成一圈，伴着幻想曲，

  满心温暖，面容如花，

  我们举酒向新娘新郎祝福，

祝福他们能拥有很多欢乐的日子。

请不要责怪我，倘若

  我猜想有一个沉默的客人[†]，

  或许，或许，在所有人中间，

尽管他沉默，也衷心在祝福。

> *指哈勒姆。

但他们必须要走了,时间快到了,
　　那令人喜爱的白色马车在等待;
　　他们起身,又徘徊;太晚了;
再会,我们亲吻,他们出发。

一道阴影落在我们中间如同暮色
　　从无云的天空落在草地上,
　　但一闪而过,于是我们也来到外面,
在林间和公园里信步而行,

谈论他们求婚的过程,
　　再说起其他已婚的人,
　　还有她的样子,他说过的话,
直到被露水打湿,才欣然回返。

筵席再启,演说,合唱,
　　从脑海拂过的阴影,
　　妙语连珠,祝他们兴旺,
香槟塔,一次次的欢呼,

还有持续的舞会;—— 直到我筋疲力竭地离开:
　　曾发出洪亮钟声的塔楼也哑默了,

高天上流云飞度,
丘陵上升起一抹微光:

月亮啊,请升起来吧,自远处的丘陵,
　　整个晚上,光亮的雾气
　　在丘陵和山谷的上方飞过,
又穿过沉默的灯火通明的城镇,

穿过粉刷过的大厅,一闪而过的小溪,
　　试图抓住每一处山巅,
　　再越过那些纵横交织的河汊,
它们寂静的银波在山陵间闪耀;

再用云影去轻触新娘的房门,
　　温柔地照耀屋顶,和墙壁;
　　再破窗而入,把光辉倾泻
在他们所休憩的每一处

幸福的海滨,涛声阵阵,
　　星辰与银河倒转,
　　一个灵魂将从无限中被唤起
将他的存在投入凡胎[*],

* 指新婚之夜将孕育出的孩子。

再经过生命最初阶段的运动,

 孕育为人,出生,思考,

 行动和爱,一种更亲密的联系

产生在我们和这些最高的种族之间,

他们心有灵犀地旁观

 人类的知识,地球上的一切

 都在他们的掌控,而在他们手中

自然就宛若一本打开的书;

那些潜藏的兽性不复存在,

 因为所有我们思考过、爱过和做过的,

 以及希望过,和经受过的,都不过是

在最高者那里开花结果后的种子;

关于那个人,那个曾和我一起

 行走在这个星球的人,是在时间成熟之前

 所出现的一个高贵典范,

我的朋友与上帝同在,

那永在的和永爱着的上帝,

 一个上帝,一条律法,一种元素,

一次遥远的神圣的事件，
宇宙万物都朝着它运动不息。

In Memoriam

PROLOGUE

Strong Son of God, immortal Love,
    Whom we, that have not seen thy face,
    By faith, and faith alone, embrace,
Believing where we cannot prove;

Thine are these orbs of light and shade;
    Thou madest Life in man and brute;
    Thou madest Death; and lo, thy foot
Is on the skull which thou hast made.

Thou wilt not leave us in the dust:
    Thou madest man, he knows not why,
    He thinks he was not made to die;
And thou hast made him: thou art just.

Thou seemest human and divine,
    The highest, holiest manhood, thou.
    Our wills are ours, we know not how;
Our wills are ours, to make them thine.

Our little systems have their day;
    They have their day and cease to be:
    They are but broken lights of thee,
And thou, O Lord, art more than they.

We have but faith: we cannot know;
    For knowledge is of things we see
    And yet we trust it comes from thee,
A beam in darkness: let it grow.

Let knowledge grow from more to more,
    But more of reverence in us dwell;
    That mind and soul, according well,
May make one music as before,

But vaster. We are fools and slight;
    We mock thee when we do not fear:
    But help thy foolish ones to bear;
Help thy vain worlds to bear thy light.

Forgive what seem'd my sin in me;
    What seem'd my worth since I began;

    For merit lives from man to man,
And not from man, O Lord, to thee.

Forgive my grief for one removed,
    Thy creature, whom I found so fair.
    I trust he lives in thee, and there
I find him worthier to be loved.

Forgive these wild and wandering cries,
    Confusions of a wasted youth;
    Forgive them where they fail in truth,
And in thy wisdom make me wise.

1849

IN MEMORIAM
A.H.H
Obiit MDCCCXXXIII

I

I held it truth, with him who sings
    To one clear harp in divers tones,
    That men may rise on stepping-stones
Of their dead selves to higher things.

But who shall so forecast the years
    And find in loss a gain to match?
    Or reach a hand thro' time to catch
The far-off interest of tears?

Let Love clasp Grief lest both be drown'd,
    Let darkness keep her raven gloss:
    Ah, sweeter to be drunk with loss,
To dance with death, to beat the ground,

Than that the victor Hours should scorn
    The long result of love, and boast,
    'Behold the man that loved and lost,
But all he was is overworn.'

II

Old Yew, which graspest at the stones
    That name the under-lying dead,
    Thy fibres net the dreamless head,
Thy roots are wrapt about the bones.

The seasons bring the flower again,
    And bring the firstling to the flock;
    And in the dusk of thee, the clock
Beats out the little lives of men.

O not for thee the glow, the bloom,
    Who changest not in any gale,
    Nor branding summer suns avail
To touch thy thousand years of gloom:

And gazing on thee, sullen tree,
    Sick for thy stubborn hardihood,
    I seem to fail from out my blood
And grow incorporate into thee.

III

O sorrow, cruel fellowship,
    O priestess in the vaults of Death,
    O sweet and bitter in a breath,
What whispers from thy lying lip?

'The stars,' she whispers, 'blindly run;
    A web is woven across the sky;
    From out waste places comes a cry,
And murmurs from the dying sun:

'And all the phantom, Nature, stands——
    With all the music in her tone,
    A hollow echo of my own, ——
A hollow form with empty hands.'

And shall I take a thing so blind,
    Embrace her as my natural good;
    Or crush her, like a vice of blood,
Upon the threshold of the mind?

IV

To sleep I give my power away;
    My will is bondsman to the dark;
    I sit within a helmless bark,
And with my heart I muse and say:

O heart, how fares it with thee now,
    That thou should'st fail from thy desire,
    Who scarcely darest to inquire,
'What is it makes me beat so low?'

Something it is which thou hast lost,
    Some pleasure from thine early years.
    Break, thou deep vase of chilling tears,
That grief hath shaken into frost,

Such clouds of nameless trouble cross
    All night below the darken'd eyes;
    With morning wakes the will, and cries,
'Thou shalt not be the fool of loss.'

V

I sometimes hold it half a sin
   To put in words the grief I feel;
   For words, like Nature, half reveal
And half conceal the Soul within.

But, for the unquiet heart and brain,
   A use in measured language lies;
   The sad mechanic exercise,
Like dull narcotics, numbing pain.

In words, like weeds, I'll wrap me o'er,
   Like coarsest clothes against the cold;
   But that large grief which these enfold
Is given outline and no more.

VI

One writes, that 'Other friends remain,'
   That 'Loss is common to the race' —
   And common is the commonplace,
And vacant chaff well meant for grain.

That loss is common would not make
   My own less bitter, rather more:
   Too common! Never morning wore
To evening, but some heart did break.

O father, wheresoe'er thou be,
   Who pledgest now thy gallant son;
   A shot, ere half thy draught be done,
Hath still'd the life that beat from thee.

O mother, praying God will save
   Thy sailor, —while thy head is bow'd,
   His heavy-shotted hammock-shroud
Drops in his vast and wandering grave.

Ye know no more than I who wrought
    At that last hour to please him well;
    Who mused on all I had to tell,
And something written, something thought;

Expecting still his advent home;
    And ever met him on his way
    With wishes, thinking, 'here to-day,'
Or 'here to-morrow will he come.'

O somewhere, meek, unconscious dove,
    That sittest ranging golden hair;
    And glad to find thyself so fair,
Poor child, that waitest for thy love!

For now her father's chimney glows
    In expectation of a guest;
    And thinking 'this will please him best,'
She takes a riband or a rose;

For he will see them on to-night;
    And with the thought her colour burns;

And, having left the glass, she turns
Once more to set a ringlet right;

And, even when she turn'd, the curse
    Had fallen, and her future Lord
    Was drown'd in passing thro' the ford,
Or kill'd in falling from his horse.

O what to her shall be the end?
    And what to me remains of good?
    To her, perpetual maidenhood,
And unto me no second friend.

VII

Dark house, by which once more I stand
    Here in the long unlovely street,
    Doors, where my heart was used to beat
So quickly, waiting for a hand,

A hand that can be clasp'd no more—
    Behold me, for I cannot sleep,
    And like a guilty thing I creep
At earliest morning to the door.

He is not here; but far away
    The noise of life begins again,
    And ghastly thro' the drizzling rain
On the bald street breaks the blank day.

VIII

A happy lover who has come
    To look on her that loves him well,
    Who 'lights and rings the gateway bell,
And learns her gone and far from home;

He saddens, all the magic light
    Dies off at once from bower and hall,
    And all the place is dark, and all
The chambers emptied of delight:

So find I every pleasant spot
    In which we two were wont to meet,
    The field, the chamber, and the street,
For all is dark where thou art not.

Yet as that other, wandering there
    In those deserted walks, may find
    A flower beat with rain and wind,
Which once she foster'd up with care;

So seems it in my deep regret,
   O my forsaken heart, with thee
   And this poor flower of poesy
Which little cared for fades not yet.

But since it pleased a vanish'd eye,
   I go to plant it on his tomb,
   That if it can it there may bloom,
Or, dying, there at least may die.

IX

Fair ship, that from the Italian shore
    Sailest the placid ocean-plains
    With my lost Arthur's loved remains,
Spread thy full wings, and waft him o'er.

So draw him home to those that mourn
    In vain; a favourable speed
    Ruffle thy mirror'd mast, and lead
Thro' prosperous floods his holy urn.

All night no ruder air perplex
    Thy sliding keel, till Phosphor, bright
    As our pure love, thro' early light
Shall glimmer on the dewy decks.

Sphere all your lights around, above;
    Sleep, gentle heavens, before the prow;
    Sleep, gentle winds, as he sleeps now,
My friend, the brother of my love;

My Arthur, whom I shall not see
   Till all my widow'd race be run;
   Dear as the mother to the son,
More than my brothers are to me.

X

I hear the noise about thy keel;
    I hear the bell struck in the night:
    I see the cabin-window bright;
I see the sailor at the wheel.

Thou bring'st the sailor to his wife,
    And travell'd men from foreign lands;
    And letters unto trembling hands;
And, thy dark freight, a vanish'd life.

So bring him; we have idle dreams:
    This look of quiet flatters thus
    Our home-bred fancies. O to us,
The fools of habit, sweeter seems

To rest beneath the clover sod,
    That takes the sunshine and the rains,
    Or where the kneeling hamlet drains
The chalice of the grapes of God;

Than if with thee the roaring wells
    Should gulf him fathom-deep in brine;
    And hands so often clasp'd in mine,
Should toss with tangle and with shells.

XI

Calm is the morn without a sound,
    Calm as to suit a calmer grief,
    And only thro' the faded leaf
The chestnut pattering to the ground:

Calm and deep peace on this high wold,
    And on these dews that drench the furze,
    And all the silvery gossamers
That twinkle into green and gold:

Calm and still light on yon great plain
    That sweeps with all its autumn bowers,
    And crowded farms and lessening towers,
To mingle with the bounding main:

Calm and deep peace in this wide air,
    These leaves that redden to the fall;
    And in my heart, if calm at all,
If any calm, a calm despair:

Calm on the seas, and silver sleep,
    And waves that sway themselves in rest,
    And dead calm in that noble breast
Which heaves but with the heaving deep.

XII

Lo, as a dove when up she springs
    To bear thro' Heaven a tale of woe,
    Some dolorous message knit below
The wild pulsation of her wings;

Like her I go; I cannot stay;
    I leave this mortal ark behind,
    A weight of nerves without a mind,
And leave the cliffs, and haste away

O'er ocean-mirrors rounded large,
    And reach the glow of southern skies,
    And see the sails at distance rise,
And linger weeping on the marge,

And saying; 'Comes he thus, my friend?
    Is this the end of all my care?'
    And circle moaning in the air:
'Is this the end? Is this the end?'

And forward dart again, and play
    About the prow, and back return
    To where the body sits, and learn
That I have been an hour away.

XIII

Tears of the widower, when he sees
    A late-lost form that sleep reveals,
    And moves his doubtful arms, and feels
Her place is empty, fall like these;

Which weep a loss for ever new,
    A void where heart on heart reposed;
    And, where warm hands have prest and closed,
Silence, till I be silent too.

Which weep the comrade of my choice,
    An awful thought, a life removed,
    The human-hearted man I loved,
A Spirit, not a breathing voice.

Come Time, and teach me, many years,
    I do not suffer in a dream;
    For now so strange do these things seem,
Mine eyes have leisure for their tears;

My fancies time to rise on wing,

    And glance about the approaching sails,

    As tho' they brought but merchants' bales,

And not the burthen that they bring.

XIV

If one should bring me this report,
    That thou hadst touch'd the land to-day,
    And I went down unto the quay,
And found thee lying in the port;

And standing, muffled round with woe,
    Should see thy passengers in rank
    Come stepping lightly down the plank,
And beckoning unto those they know;

And if along with these should come
    The man I held as half-divine;
    Should strike a sudden hand in mine,
And ask a thousand things of home;

And I should tell him all my pain,
    And how my life had droop'd of late,
    And he should sorrow o'er my state
And marvel what possess'd my brain;

And I perceived no touch of change,
    No hint of death in all his frame,
    But found him all in all the same,
I should not feel it to be strange.

XV

To-night the winds begin to rise
    And roar from yonder dropping day:
    The last red leaf is whirl'd away,
The rooks are blown about the skies;

The forest crack'd, the waters curl'd,
    The cattle huddled on the lea;
    And wildly dash'd on tower and tree
The sunbeam strikes along the world:

And but for fancies, which aver
    That all thy motions gently pass
    Athwart a plane of molten glass,
I scarce could brook the strain and stir

That makes the barren branches loud;
    And but for fear it is not so,
    The wild unrest that lives in woe
Would dote and pore on yonder cloud

That rises upward always higher,
    And onward drags a labouring breast,
    And topples round the dreary west,
A looming bastion fringed with fire.

XVI

What words are these have fall'n from me?
    Can calm despair and wild unrest
    Be tenants of a single breast,
Or sorrow such a changeling be?

Or doth she only seem to take
    The touch of change in calm or storm;
    But knows no more of transient form
In her deep self, than some dead lake

That holds the shadow of a lark
    Hung in the shadow of a heaven?
    Or has the shock, so harshly given,
Confused me like the unhappy bark

That strikes by night a craggy shelf,
    And staggers blindly ere she sink?
    And stunn'd me from my power to think
And all my knowledge of myself;

And made me that delirious man
    Whose fancy fuses old and new,
    And flashes into false and true,
And mingles all without a plan?

XVII

Thou comest, much wept for: such a breeze
    Compell'd thy canvas, and my prayer
    Was as the whisper of an air
To breathe thee over lonely seas.

For I in spirit saw thee move
    Thro' circles of the bounding sky,
    Week after week: the days go by:
Come quick, thou bringest all I love.

Henceforth, wherever thou may'st roam,
    My blessing, like a line of light,
    Is on the waters day and night,
And like a beacon guards thee home.

So may whatever tempest mars
    Mid-ocean, spare thee, sacred bark;
    And balmy drops in summer dark
Slide from the bosom of the stars.

So kind an office hath been done,
>   Such precious relics brought by thee;
>   The dust of him I shall not see
Till all my widow'd race be run.

XVIII

'Tis well; 'tis something; we may stand
   Where he in English earth is laid,
   And from his ashes may be made
The violet of his native land.

'Tis little; but it looks in truth
   As if the quiet bones were blest
   Among familiar names to rest
And in the places of his youth.

Come then, pure hands, and bear the head
   That sleeps or wears the mask of sleep,
   And come, whatever loves to weep,
And hear the ritual of the dead.

Ah yet, ev'n yet, if this might be,
   I, falling on his faithful heart,
   Would breathing thro' his lips impart
The life that almost dies in me;

That dies not, but endures with pain,
    And slowly forms the firmer mind,
    Treasuring the look it cannot find,
The words that are not heard again.

XIX

The Danube to the Severn gave
    The darken'd heart that beat no more;
    They laid him by the pleasant shore,
And in the hearing of the wave.

There twice a day the Severn fills;
    The salt sea-water passes by,
    And hushes half the babbling Wye,
And makes a silence in the hills.

The Wye is hush'd nor moved along,
    And hush'd my deepest grief of all,
    When fill'd with tears that cannot fall,
I brim with sorrow drowning song.

The tide flows down, the wave again
    Is vocal in its wooded walls;
    My deeper anguish also falls,
And I can speak a little then.

XX

The lesser griefs that may be said,
    That breathe a thousand tender vows,
    Are but as servants in a house
Where lies the master newly dead;

Who speak their feeling as it is,
    And weep the fulness from the mind:
    'It will be hard,' they say, 'to find
Another service such as this.'

My lighter moods are like to these,
    That out of words a comfort win;
    But there are other griefs within,
And tears that at their fountain freeze;

For by the hearth the children sit
    Cold in that atmosphere of Death,
    And scarce endure to draw the breath,
Or like to noiseless phantoms flit;

But open converse is there none,
    So much the vital spirits sink
    To see the vacant chair, and think,
'How good! how kind! and he is gone.'

XXI

I sing to him that rests below,
    And, since the grasses round me wave,
    I take the grasses of the grave,
And make them pipes whereon to blow.

The traveller hears me now and then,
    And sometimes harshly will he speak:
    'This fellow would make weakness weak,
And melt the waxen hearts of men.'

Another answers, 'Let him be,
    He loves to make parade of pain
    That with his piping he may gain
The praise that comes to constancy.'

A third is wroth: 'Is this an hour
    For private sorrow's barren song,
    When more and more the people throng
The chairs and thrones of civil power?

'A time to sicken and to swoon,
   When Science reaches forth her arms
   To feel from world to world, and charms
Her secret from the latest moon?'

Behold, ye speak an idle thing:
   Ye never knew the sacred dust:
   I do but sing because I must,
And pipe but as the linnets sing:

And one is glad; her note is gay,
   For now her little ones have ranged;
   And one is sad; her note is changed,
Because her brood is stol'n away.

XXII

The path by which we twain did go,
    Which led by tracts that pleased us well,
    Thro' four sweet years arose and fell,
From flower to flower, from snow to snow:

And we with singing cheer'd the way,
    And, crown'd with all the season lent,
    From April on to April went,
And glad at heart from May to May:

But where the path we walk'd began
    To slant the fifth autumnal slope,
    As we descended following Hope,
There sat the Shadow fear'd of man;

Who broke our fair companionship,
    And spread his mantle dark and cold,
    And wrapt thee formless in the fold,
And dull'd the murmur on thy lip,

And bore thee where I could not see
    Nor follow, tho' I walk in haste,
    And think, that somewhere in the waste
The Shadow sits and waits for me.

XXIII

Now, sometimes in my sorrow shut,
   Or breaking into song by fits;
   Alone, alone, to where he sits,
The Shadow cloak'd from head to foot,

Who keeps the keys of all the creeds,
   I wander, often falling lame,
   And looking back to whence I came,
Or on to where the pathway leads;

And crying, How changed from where it ran
   Thro' lands where not a leaf was dumb;
   But all the lavish hills would hum
The murmur of a happy Pan.

When each by turns was guide to each,
   And Fancy light from Fancy caught,
   And Thought leapt out to wed with Thought
Ere Thought could wed itself with Speech;

And all we met was fair and good,
    And all was good that Time could bring,
    And all the secret of the Spring
Moved in the chambers of the blood;

And many an old philosophy
    On Argive heights divinely sang,
    And round us all the thicket rang
To many a flute of Arcady.

XXIV

And was the day of my delight
    As pure and perfect as I say?
    The very source and fount of Day
Is dash'd with wandering isles of night.

If all was good and fair we met,
    This earth had been the Paradise
    It never look'd to human eyes
Since our first Sun arose and set.

And is it that the haze of grief
    Makes former gladness loom so great?
    The lowness of the present state,
That sets the past in this relief?

Or that the past will always win
    A glory from its being far;
    And orb into the perfect star
We saw not, when we moved therein?

XXV

I know that this was Life, —the track
    Whereon with equal feet we fared;
    And then, as now, the day prepared
The daily burden for the back.

But this it was that made me move
    As light as carrier-birds in air;
    I loved the weight I had to bear,
Because it needed help of Love:

Nor could I weary, heart or limb,
    When mighty Love would cleave in twain
    The lading of a single pain,
And part it, giving half to him.

XXVI

Still onward winds the dreary way;
    I with it; for I long to prove
    No lapse of moons can canker Love,
Whatever fickle tongues may say.

And if that eye which watches guilt
    And goodness, and hath power to see
    Within the green the moulder'd tree,
And towers fall'n as soon as built—

Oh, if indeed that eye foresee
    Or see (in Him is no before)
    In more of life true life no more
And Love the indifference to be,

Then might I find, ere yet the morn
    Breaks hither over Indian seas,
    That Shadow waiting with the keys,
To shroud me from my proper scorn.

XXVII

I envy not in any moods
    The captive void of noble rage,
    The linnet born within the cage,
That never knew the summer woods:

I envy not the beast that takes
    His license in the field of time,
    Unfetter'd by the sense of crime,
To whom a conscience never wakes;

Nor, what may count itself as blest,
    The heart that never plighted troth
    But stagnates in the weeds of sloth;
Nor any want-begotten rest.

I hold it true, whate'er befall;
    I feel it, when I sorrow most;
    'Tis better to have loved and lost
Than never to have loved at all.

XXVIII

The time draws near the birth of Christ:
    The moon is hid; the night is still;
    The Christmas bells from hill to hill
Answer each other in the mist.

Four voices of four hamlets round,
    From far and near, on mead and moor,
    Swell out and fail, as if a door
Were shut between me and the sound:

Each voice four changes on the wind,
    That now dilate, and now decrease,
    Peace and goodwill, goodwill and peace,
Peace and goodwill, to all mankind.

This year I slept and woke with pain,
    I almost wish'd no more to wake,
    And that my hold on life would break
Before I heard those bells again:

But they my troubled spirit rule,
    For they controll'd me when a boy;
    They bring me sorrow touch'd with joy,
The merry merry bells of Yule.

XXIX

With such compelling cause to grieve
    As daily vexes household peace,
    And chains regret to his decease,
How dare we keep our Christmas-eve;

Which brings no more a welcome guest
    To enrich the threshold of the night
    With shower'd largess of delight
In dance and song and game and jest?

Yet go, and while the holly boughs
    Entwine the cold baptismal font,
    Make one wreath more for Use and Wont,
That guard the portals of the house;

Old sisters of a day gone by,
    Gray nurses, loving nothing new;
    Why should they miss their yearly due
Before their time? They too will die.

XXX

With trembling fingers did we weave
    The holly round the Chrismas hearth;
    A rainy cloud possess'd the earth,
And sadly fell our Christmas-eve.

At our old pastimes in the hall
    We gambol'd, making vain pretence
    Of gladness, with an awful sense
Of one mute Shadow watching all.

We paused: the winds were in the beech:
    We heard them sweep the winter land;
    And in a circle hand-in-hand
Sat silent, looking each at each.

Then echo-like our voices rang;
    We sung, tho' every eye was dim,
    A merry song we sang with him
Last year: impetuously we sang:

We ceased: a gentler feeling crept
    Upon us: surely rest is meet:
    'They rest,' we said, 'their sleep is sweet,'
And silence follow'd, and we wept.

Our voices took a higher range;
    Once more we sang: 'They do not die
    Nor lose their mortal sympathy,
Nor change to us, although they change;

'Rapt from the fickle and the frail
    With gather'd power, yet the same,
    Pierces the keen seraphic flame
From orb to orb, from veil to veil.'

Rise, happy morn, rise, holy morn,
    Draw forth the cheerful day from night:
    O Father, touch the east, and light
The light that shone when Hope was born.

XXXI

When Lazarus left his charnel-cave,
    And home to Mary's house return'd,
    Was this demanded - if he yearn'd
To hear her weeping by his grave?

'Where wert thou, brother, those four days?'
    There lives no record of reply,
    Which telling what it is to die
Had surely added praise to praise.

From every house the neighbours met,
    The streets were fill'd with joyful sound,
    A solemn gladness even crown'd
The purple brows of Olivet.

Behold a man raised up by Christ!
    The rest remaineth unreveal'd;
    He told it not; or something seal'd
The lips of that Evangelist.

XXXII

Her eyes are homes of silent prayer,
    Nor other thought her mind admits
    But, he was dead, and there he sits,
And he that brought him back is there.

Then one deep love doth supersede
    All other, when her ardent gaze
    Roves from the living brother's face,
And rests upon the Life indeed.

All subtle thought, all curious fears,
    Borne down by gladness so complete,
    She bows, she bathes the Saviour's feet
With costly spikenard and with tears.

Thrice blest whose lives are faithful prayers,
    Whose loves in higher love endure;
    What souls possess themselves so pure,
Or is there blessedness like theirs?

XXXIII

O thou that after toil and storm
    Mayst seem to have reach'd a purer air,
    Whose faith has centre everywhere,
Nor cares to fix itself to form,

Leave thou thy sister when she prays,
    Her early Heaven, her happy views;
    Nor thou with shadow'd hint confuse
A life that leads melodious days.

Her faith thro' form is pure as thine,
    Her hands are quicker unto good:
    Oh, sacred be the flesh and blood
To which she links a truth divine!

See thou, that countest reason ripe
    In holding by the law within,
    Thou fail not in a world of sin,
And ev'n for want of such a type.

XXXIV

My own dim life should teach me this,
    That life shall live for evermore,
    Else earth is darkness at the core,
And dust and ashes all that is;

This round of green, this orb of flame,
    Fantastic beauty; such as lurks
    In some wild Poet, when he works
Without a conscience or an aim.

What then were God to such as I?
    'Twere hardly worth my while to choose
    Of things all mortal, or to use
A little patience ere I die;

'Twere best at once to sink to peace,
    Like birds the charming serpent draws,
    To drop head-foremost in the jaws
Of vacant darkness and to cease.

XXXV

Yet if some voice that man could trust
    Should murmur from the narrow house,
    'The cheeks drop in; the body bows;
Man dies: nor is there hope in dust:'

Might I not say? 'Yet even here,
    But for one hour, O Love, I strive
    To keep so sweet a thing alive:'
But I should turn mine ears and hear

The moanings of the homeless sea,
    The sound of streams that swift or slow
    Draw down Aeonian hills, and sow
The dust of continents to be;

And Love would answer with a sigh,
    'The sound of that forgetful shore
    Will change my sweetness more and more,
Half-dead to know that I shall die.'

O me, what profits it to put
    An idle case? If Death were seen
    At first as Death, Love had not been,
Or been in narrowest working shut,

Mere fellowship of sluggish moods,
    Or in his coarsest Satyr-shape
    Had bruised the herb and crush'd the grape,
And bask'd and batten'd in the woods.

XXXVI

Tho' truths in manhood darkly join,
    Deep-seated in our mystic frame,
    We yield all blessing to the name
Of Him that made them current coin;

For Wisdom dealt with mortal powers,
    Where truth in closest words shall fail,
    When truth embodied in a tale
Shall enter in at lowly doors.

And so the Word had breath, and wrought
    With human hands the creed of creeds
    In loveliness of perfect deeds,
More strong than all poetic thought;

Which he may read that binds the sheaf,
    Or builds the house, or digs the grave,
    And those wild eyes that watch the wave
In roarings round the coral reef.

XXXVII

Urania speaks with darken'd brow:
    'Thou pratest here where thou art least;
    This faith has many a purer priest,
And many an abler voice than thou.

'Go down beside thy native rill,
    On thy Parnassus set thy feet,
    And hear thy laurel whisper sweet
About the ledges of the hill.'

And my Melpomene replies,
    A touch of shame upon her cheek:
    'I am not worthy ev'n to speak
Of thy prevailing mysteries;

'For I am but an earthly Muse,
    And owning but a little art
    To lull with song an aching heart,
And render human love his dues;

'But brooding on the dear one dead,
    And all he said of things divine,
    (And dear to me as sacred wine
To dying lips is all he said),

'I murmur'd, as I came along,
    Of comfort clasp'd in truth reveal'd;
    And loiter'd in the master's field,
And darken'd sanctities with song.'

XXXVIII

With weary steps I loiter on,
    Tho' always under alter'd skies
    The purple from the distance dies,
My prospect and horizon gone.

No joy the blowing season gives,
    The herald melodies of spring,
    But in the songs I love to sing
A doubtful gleam of solace lives.

If any care for what is here
    Survive in spirits render'd free,
    Then are these songs I sing of thee
Not all ungrateful to thine ear.

XXXIX

Old warder of these buried bones,
    And answering now my random stroke
    With fruitful cloud and living smoke,
Dark yew, that graspest at the stones

And dippest toward the dreamless head,
    To thee too comes the golden hour
    When flower is feeling after flower;
But Sorrow—fixt upon the dead,

And darkening the dark graves of men,—
    What whisper'd from her lying lips?
    Thy gloom is kindled at the tips,
And passes into gloom again.

XL

Could we forget the widow'd hour
    And look on Spirits breathed away,
    As on a maiden in the day
When first she wears her orange-flower!

When crown'd with blessing she doth rise
    To take her latest leave of home,
    And hopes and light regrets that come
Make April of her tender eyes;

And doubtful joys the father move,
    And tears are on the mother's face,
    As parting with a long embrace
She enters other realms of love;

Her office there to rear, to teach,
    Becoming as is meet and fit
    A link among the days, to knit
The generations each with each;

And, doubtless, unto thee is given
    A life that bears immortal fruit
    In those great offices that suit
The full-grown energies of heaven.

Ay me, the difference I discern!
    How often shall her old fireside
    Be cheer'd with tidings of the bride,
How often she herself return,

And tell them all they would have told,
    And bring her babe, and make her boast,
    Till even those that miss'd her most
Shall count new things as dear as old:

But thou and I have shaken hands,
    Till growing winters lay me low;
    My paths are in the fields I know.
And thine in undiscover'd lands.

XLI

Thy spirit ere our fatal loss
    Did ever rise from high to higher;
    As mounts the heavenward altar-fire,
As flies the lighter thro' the gross.

But thou art turn'd to something strange,
    And I have lost the links that bound
    Thy changes; here upon the ground,
No more partaker of thy change.

Deep folly! yet that this could be—
    That I could wing my will with might
    To leap the grades of life and light,
And flash at once, my friend, to thee.

For tho' my nature rarely yields
    To that vague fear implied in death;
    Nor shudders at the gulfs beneath,
The howlings from forgotten fields;

Yet oft when sundown skirts the moor
    An inner trouble I behold,
    A spectral doubt which makes me cold,
That I shall be thy mate no more,

Tho' following with an upward mind
    The wonders that have come to thee,
    Thro' all the secular to-be,
But evermore a life behind.

XLII

I vex my heart with fancies dim:
    He still outstript me in the race;
    It was but unity of place
That made me dream I rank'd with him.

And so may Place retain us still,
    And he the much-beloved again,
    A lord of large experience, train
To riper growth the mind and will:

And what delights can equal those
    That stir the spirit's inner deeps,
    When one that loves but knows not, reaps
A truth from one that loves and knows?

XLIII

If Sleep and Death be truly one,
    And every spirit's folded bloom
    Thro' all its intervital gloom
In some long trance should slumber on;

Unconscious of the sliding hour,
    Bare of the body, might it last,
    And silent traces of the past
Be all the colour of the flower:

So then were nothing lost to man;
    So that still garden of the souls
    In many a figured leaf enrolls
The total world since life began;

And love will last as pure and whole
    As when he loved me here in Time,
    And at the spiritual prime
Rewaken with the dawning soul.

XLIV

How fares it with the happy dead?
    For here the man is more and more;
    But he forgets the days before
God shut the doorways of his head.

The days have vanish'd, tone and tint,
    And yet perhaps the hoarding sense
    Gives out at times (he knows not whence)
A little flash, a mystic hint;

And in the long harmonious years
    (If Death so taste Lethean springs),
    May some dim touch of earthly things
Surprise thee ranging with thy peers.

If such a dreamy touch should fall,
    O turn thee round, resolve the doubt;
    My guardian angel will speak out
In that high place, and tell thee all.

XLV

The baby new to earth and sky,
    What time his tender palm is prest
    Against the circle of the breast,
Has never thought that 'this is I:'

But as he grows he gathers much,
    And learns the use of 'I', and 'me,'
    And finds 'I am not what I see,
And other than the things I touch.'

So rounds he to a separate mind
    From whence clear memory may begin,
    As thro' the frame that binds him in
His isolation grows defined.

This use may lie in blood and breath,
    Which else were fruitless of their due,
    Had man to learn himself anew
Beyond the second birth of Death.

XLVI

We ranging down this lower track,
    The path we came by, thorn and flower,
    Is shadow'd by the growing hour,
Lest life should fail in looking back.

So be it: there no shade can last
    In that deep dawn behind the tomb,
    But clear from marge to marge shall bloom
The eternal landscape of the past;

A lifelong tract of time reveal'd;
    The fruitful hours of still increase;
    Days order'd in a wealthy peace,
And those five years its richest field.

O Love, thy province were not large,
    A bounded field, nor stretching far;
    Look also, Love, a brooding star,
A rosy warmth from marge to marge.

XLVII

That each, who seems a separate whole,
    Should move his rounds, and fusing all
    The skirts of self again, should fall
Remerging in the general Soul,

Is faith as vague as all unsweet:
    Eternal form shall still divide
    The eternal soul from all beside;
And I shall know him when we meet:

And we shall sit at endless feast,
    Enjoying each the other's good:
    What vaster dream can hit the mood
Of Love on earth? He seeks at least

Upon the last and sharpest height,
    Before the spirits fade away,
    Some landing-place, to clasp and say,
'Farewell! We lose ourselves in light.'

XLVIII

If these brief lays, of Sorrow born,
    Were taken to be such as closed
    Grave doubts and answers here proposed,
Then these were such as men might scorn:

Her care is not to part and prove;
    She takes, when harsher moods remit,
    What slender shade of doubt may flit,
And makes it vassal unto love:

And hence, indeed, she sports with words,
    But better serves a wholesome law,
    And holds it sin and shame to draw
The deepest measure from the chords:

Nor dare she trust a larger lay,
    But rather loosens from the lip
    Short swallow-flights of song, that dip
Their wings in tears, and skim away.

XLIX

From art, from nature, from the schools,
    Let random influences glance,
    Like light in many a shiver'd lance
That breaks about the dappled pools:

The lightest wave of thought shall lisp,
    The fancy's tenderest eddy wreathe,
    The slightest air of song shall breathe
To make the sullen surface crisp.

And look thy look, and go thy way,
    But blame not thou the winds that make
    The seeming-wanton ripple break,
The tender-pencil'd shadow play.

Beneath all fancied hopes and fears
    Ay me, the sorrow deepens down,
    Whose muffled motions blindly drown
The bases of my life in tears.

L

Be near me when my light is low,
>   When the blood creeps, and the nerves prick
>   And tingle; and the heart is sick,
And all the wheels of Being slow.

Be near me when the sensuous frame
>   Is rack'd with pangs that conquer trust;
>   And Time, a maniac scattering dust,
And Life, a Fury slinging flame.

Be near me when my faith is dry,
>   And men the flies of latter spring,
>   That lay their eggs, and sting and sing
And weave their petty cells and die.

Be near me when I fade away,
>   To point the term of human strife,
>   And on the low dark verge of life
The twilight of eternal day.

LI

Do we indeed desire the dead
    Should still be near us at our side?
    Is there no baseness we would hide?
No inner vileness that we dread?

Shall he for whose applause I strove,
    I had such reverence for his blame,
    See with clear eye some hidden shame
And I be lessen'd in his love?

I wrong the grave with fears untrue:
    Shall love be blamed for want of faith?
    There must be wisdom with great Death:
The dead shall look me thro' and thro'.

Be near us when we climb or fall:
    Ye watch, like God, the rolling hours
    With larger other eyes than ours,
To make allowance for us all.

LII

I cannot love thee as I ought,
    For love reflects the thing beloved;
    My words are only words, and moved
Upon the topmost froth of thought.

'Yet blame not thou thy plaintive song,'
    The Spirit of true love replied;
    'Thou canst not move me from thy side,
Nor human frailty do me wrong.

'What keeps a spirit wholly true
    To that ideal which he bears?
    What record? not the sinless years
That breathed beneath the Syrian blue:

'So fret not, like an idle girl,
    That life is dash'd with flecks of sin.
    Abide: thy wealth is gather'd in,
When Time hath sunder'd shell from pearl.'

LIII

How many a father have I seen,
    A sober man, among his boys,
    Whose youth was full of foolish noise,
Who wears his manhood hale and green:

And dare we to this fancy give,
    That had the wild oat not been sown,
    The soil, left barren, scarce had grown
The grain by which a man may live?

Or, if we held the doctrine sound
    For life outliving heats of youth,
    Yet who would preach it as a truth
To those that eddy round and round?

Hold thou the good: define it well:
    For fear divine Philosophy
    Should push beyond her mark, and be
Procuress to the Lords of Hell.

LIV

Oh yet we trust that somehow good
   Will be the final goal of ill,
   To pangs of nature, sins of will,
Defects of doubt, and taints of blood;

That nothing walks with aimless feet;
   That not one life shall be destroy'd,
   Or cast as rubbish to the void,
When God hath made the pile complete;

That not a worm is cloven in vain;
   That not a moth with vain desire
   Is shrivell'd in a fruitless fire,
Or but subserves another's gain.

Behold, we know not anything;
   I can but trust that good shall fall
   At last—far off—at last, to all,
And every winter change to spring.

So runs my dream: but what am I?

    An infant crying in the night:

    An infant crying for the light:

And with no language but a cry.

LV

The wish, that of the living whole
    No life may fail beyond the grave,
    Derives it not from what we have
The likest God within the soul?

Are God and Nature then at strife,
    That Nature lends such evil dreams?
    So careful of the type she seems,
So careless of the single life;

That I, considering everywhere
    Her secret meaning in her deeds,
    And finding that of fifty seeds
She often brings but one to bear,

I falter where I firmly trod,
    And falling with my weight of cares
    Upon the great world's altar-stairs
That slope thro' darkness up to God,

I stretch lame hands of faith, and grope,
    And gather dust and chaff, and call
    To what I feel is Lord of all,
And faintly trust the larger hope.

LVI

'So careful of the type?' but no.
    From scarped cliff and quarried stone
    She cries, 'A thousand types are gone:
I care for nothing, all shall go.

'Thou makest thine appeal to me:
    I bring to life, I bring to death:
    The spirit does but mean the breath:
I know no more.' And he, shall he,

Man, her last work, who seem'd so fair,
    Such splendid purpose in his eyes,
    Who roll'd the psalm to wintry skies,
Who built him fanes of fruitless prayer,

Who trusted God was love indeed
    And love Creation's final law—
    Tho' Nature, red in tooth and claw
With ravine, shriek'd against his creed—

Who loved, who suffer'd countless ills,
 Who battled for the True, the Just,
 Be blown about the desert dust,
Or seal'd within the iron hills?

No more? A monster then, a dream,
 A discord. Dragons of the prime,
 That tare each other in their slime,
Were mellow music match'd with him.

O life as futile, then, as frail!
 O for thy voice to soothe and bless!
 What hope of answer, or redress?
Behind the veil, behind the veil.

LVII

Peace; come away: the song of woe
    Is after all an earthly song:
    Peace; come away: we do him wrong
To sing so wildly: let us go.

Come; let us go: your cheeks are pale;
    But half my life I leave behind:
    Methinks my friend is richly shrined;
But I shall pass; my work will fail.

Yet in these ears, till hearing dies,
    One set slow bell will seem to toll
    The passing of the sweetest soul
That ever look'd with human eyes.

I hear it now, and o'er and o'er
    Eternal greetings to the dead;
    And 'Ave, Ave, Ave,' said,
'Adieu, adieu' for evermore.

LVIII

In those sad words I took farewell:
    Like echoes in sepulchral halls,
    As drop by drop the water falls
In vaults and catacombs, they fell;

And, falling, idly broke the peace
    Of hearts that beat from day to day,
    Half-conscious of their dying clay,
And those cold crypts where they shall cease

The high Muse answer'd: 'Wherefore grieve
    Thy brethren with a fruitless tear?
    Abide a little longer here,
And thou shalt take a nobler leave.'

LIX

O sorrow, wilt thou live with me
    No casual mistress, but a wife,
    My bosom-friend and half of life;
As I confess it needs must be;

O Sorrow, wilt thou rule my blood,
    Be sometimes lovely like a bride,
    And put thy harsher moods aside,
If thou wilt have me wise and good.

My centred passion cannot move,
    Nor will it lessen from to-day;
    But I'll have leave at times to play
As with the creature of my love;

And set thee forth, for thou art mine,
    With so much hope for years to come,
    That, howsoe'er I know thee, some
Could hardly tell what name were thine.

LX

He past; a soul of nobler tone:
    My spirit loved and loves him yet,
    Like some poor girl whose heart is set
On one whose rank exceeds her own.

He mixing with his proper sphere,
    She finds the baseness of her lot,
    Half jealous of she knows not what,
And envying all that meet him there.

The little village looks forlorn;
    She sighs amid her narrow days,
    Moving about the household ways,
In that dark house where she was born.

The foolish neighbours come and go,
    And tease her till the day draws by:
    At night she weeps, 'How vain am I!
How should he love a thing so low?'

LXI

If, in thy second state sublime,
   Thy ransom'd reason change replies
   With all the circle of the wise,
The perfect flower of human time;

And if thou cast thine eyes below,
   How dimly character'd and slight,
   How dwarf'd a growth of cold and night,
How blanch'd with darkness must I grow!

Yet turn thee to the doubtful shore,
   Where thy first form was made a man;
   I loved thee, Spirit, and love, nor can
The soul of Shakspeare love thee more.

LXII

Tho' if an eye that's downward cast
    Could make thee somewhat blench or fail,
    Then be my love an idle tale,
And fading legend of the past;

And thou, as one that once declined,
    When he was little more than boy,
    On some unworthy heart with joy,
But lives to wed an equal mind;

And breathes a novel world, the while
    His other passion wholly dies,
    Or in the light of deeper eyes
Is matter for a flying smile.

LXIII

Yet pity for a horse o'er-driven,
    And love in which my hound has part,
    Can hang no weight upon my heart
In its assumptions up to heaven;

And I am so much more than these,
    As thou, perchance, art more than I,
    And yet I spare them sympathy,
And I would set their pains at ease.

So mayst thou watch me where I weep,
    As, unto vaster motions bound,
    The circuits of thine orbit round
A higher height, a deeper deep.

LXIV

Dost thou look back on what hath been,
    As some divinely gifted man,
    Whose life in low estate began
And on a simple village green;

Who breaks his birth's invidious bar,
    And grasps the skirts of happy chance,
    And breasts the blows of circumstance,
And grapples with his evil star;

Who makes by force his merit known
    And lives to clutch the golden keys,
    To mould a mighty state's decrees,
And shape the whisper of the throne;

And moving up from high to higher,
    Becomes on Fortune's crowning slope
    The pillar of a people's hope,
The centre of a world's desire;

Yet feels, as in a pensive dream,
    When all his active powers are still,
    A distant dearness in the hill,
A secret sweetness in the stream,

The limit of his narrower fate,
    While yet beside its vocal springs
    He play'd at counsellors and kings.
With one that was his earliest mate;

Who ploughs with pain his native lea
    And reaps the labour of his hands,
    Or in the furrow musing stands;
'Does my old friend remember me?'

LXV

Sweet soul, do with me as thou wilt;
    I lull a fancy trouble-tost
    With 'Love's too precious to be lost,
A little grain shall not be spilt.'

And in that solace can I sing,
    Till out of painful phases wrought
    There flutters up a happy thought,
Self-balanced on a lightsome wing:

Since we deserved the name of friends,
    And thine effect so lives in me,
    A part of mine may live in thee
And move thee on to noble ends.

LXVI

You thought my heart too far diseased;
    You wonder when my fancies play
    To find me gay among the gay,
Like one with any trifle pleased.

The shade by which my life was crost,
    Which makes a desert in the mind,
    Has made me kindly with my kind,
And like to him whose sight is lost;

Whose feet are guided thro' the land,
    Whose jest among his friends is free,
    Who takes the children on his knee,
And winds their curls about his hand:

He plays with threads, he beats his chair
    For pastime, dreaming of the sky;
    His inner day can never die,
His night of loss is always there.

LXVII

When on my bed the moonlight falls,
   I know that in thy place of rest
   By that broad water of the west,
There comes a glory on the walls;

Thy marble bright in dark appears,
   As slowly steals a silver flame
   Along the letters of thy name,
And o'er the number of thy years.

The mystic glory swims away;
   From off my bed the moonlight dies;
   And closing eaves of wearied eyes
I sleep till dusk is dipt in gray:

And then I know the mist is drawn
   A lucid veil from coast to coast,
   And in the dark church like a ghost
Thy tablet glimmers to the dawn.

LXVIII

When in the down I sink my head,
    Sleep, Death's twin-brother, times my breath;
    Sleep, Death's twin-brother, knows not Death,
Nor can I dream of thee as dead:

I walk as ere I walk'd forlorn,
    When all our path was fresh with dew,
    And all the bugle breezes blew
Reveillee to the breaking morn.

But what is this? I turn about,
    I find a trouble in thine eye,
    Which makes me sad I know not why,
Nor can my dream resolve the doubt:

But ere the lark hath left the lea
    I wake, and I discern the truth;
    It is the trouble of my youth
That foolish sleep transfers to thee.

LXIX

I dream'd there would be Spring no more,
    That Nature's ancient power was lost:
    The streets were black with smoke and frost,
They chatter'd trifles at the door:

I wander'd from the noisy town,
    I found a wood with thorny boughs:
    I took the thorns to bind my brows,
I wore them like a civic crown:

I met with scoffs, I met with scorns
    From youth and babe and hoary hairs:
    They call'd me in the public squares
The fool that wears a crown of thorns:

They call'd me fool, they call'd me child:
    I found an angel of the night;
    The voice was low, the look was bright;
He look'd upon my crown and smiled:

He reach'd the glory of a hand,
   That seem'd to touch it into leaf:
   The voice was not the voice of grief,
The words were hard to understand.

LXX

I cannot see the features right,
    When on the gloom I strive to paint
    The face I know; the hues are faint
And mix with hollow masks of night;

Cloud-towers by ghostly masons wrought,
    A gulf that ever shuts and gapes,
    A hand that points, and palled shapes
In shadowy thoroughfares of thought;

And crowds that stream from yawning doors,
    And shoals of pucker'd faces drive;
    Dark bulks that tumble half alive,
And lazy lengths on boundless shores;

Till all at once beyond the will
    I hear a wizard music roll,
    And thro' a lattice on the soul
Looks thy fair face and makes it still.

LXXI

Sleep, kinsman thou to death and trance
    And madness, thou hast forged at last
    A night-long Present of the Past
In which we went thro' summer France.

Hadst thou such credit with the soul?
    Then bring an opiate trebly strong,
    Drug down the blindfold sense of wrong
That so my pleasure may be whole;

While now we talk as once we talk'd
    Of men and minds, the dust of change,
    The days that grow to something strange,
In walking as of old we walk'd

Beside the river's wooded reach,
    The fortress, and the mountain ridge,
    The cataract flashing from the bridge,
The breaker breaking on the beach.

LXXII

Risest thou thus, dim dawn, again,
    And howlest, issuing out of night,
    With blasts that blow the poplar white,
And lash with storm the streaming pane?

Day, when my crown'd estate begun
    To pine in that reverse of doom,
    Which sicken'd every living bloom,
And blurr'd the splendour of the sun;

Who usherest in the dolorous hour
    With thy quick tears that make the rose
    Pull sideways, and the daisy close
Her crimson fringes to the shower;

Who might'st have heaved a windless flame
    Up the deep East, or, whispering, play'd
    A chequer-work of beam and shade
Along the hills, yet look'd the same.

As wan, as chill, as wild as now;
    Day, mark'd as with some hideous crime,
    When the dark hand struck down thro' time,
And cancell'd nature's best: but thou,

 Lift as thou may'st thy burthen'd brows
    Thro' clouds that drench the morning star,
    And whirl the ungarner'd sheaf afar,
And sow the sky with flying boughs,

And up thy vault with roaring sound
    Climb thy thick noon, disastrous day;
    Touch thy dull goal of joyless gray,
And hide thy shame beneath the ground

LXXIII

So many worlds, so much to do,
    So little done, such things to be,
    How know I what had need of thee,
For thou wert strong as thou wert true?

The fame is quench'd that I foresaw,
    The head hath miss'd an earthly wreath:
    I curse not nature, no, nor death;
For nothing is that errs from law.

We pass; the path that each man trod
    Is dim, or will be dim, with weeds:
    What fame is left for human deeds
In endless age? It rests with God.

O hollow wraith of dying fame,
    Fade wholly, while the soul exults,
    And self-infolds the large results
Of force that would have forged a name.

LXXIV

As sometimes in a dead man's face,
    To those that watch it more and more,
    A likeness, hardly seen before,
Comes out—to some one of his race:

So, dearest, now thy brows are cold,
    I see thee what thou art, and know
    Thy likeness to the wise below,
Thy kindred with the great of old.

But there is more than I can see,
    And what I see I leave unsaid,
    Nor speak it, knowing Death has made
His darkness beautiful with thee.

LXXV

I leave thy praises unexpress'd
    In verse that brings myself relief,
    And by the measure of my grief
I leave thy greatness to be guess'd;

What practice howsoe'er expert
    In fitting aptest words to things,
    Or voice the richest-toned that sings,
Hath power to give thee as thou wert?

I care not in these fading days
    To raise a cry that lasts not long,
    And round thee with the breeze of song
To stir a little dust of praise.

Thy leaf has perish'd in the green,
    And, while we breathe beneath the sun,
    The world which credits what is done
Is cold to all that might have been.

So here shall silence guard thy fame;
    But somewhere, out of human view,
    Whate'er thy hands are set to do
Is wrought with tumult of acclaim.

LXXVI

Take wings of fancy, and ascend,
    And in a moment set thy face
    Where all the starry heavens of space
Are sharpen'd to a needle's end;

Take wings of foresight; lighten thro'
    The secular abyss
    And lo, thy deepest lays are dumb
Before the mouldering of a yew,

And if the matin songs, that woke
    The darkness of our planet, last,
    Thine own shall wither in the vast,
Ere half the lifetime of an oak.

Ere these have clothed their branchy bowers
    With fifty Mays, thy songs are vain;
    And what are they when these remain
The ruin'd shells of hollow towers?

LXXVII

What hope is here for modern rhyme
    To him, who turns a musing eye
    On songs, and deeds, and lives, that lie
Foreshorten'd in the tract of time?

These mortal lullabies of pain
    May bind a book, may line a box,
    May serve to curl a maiden's locks;
Or when a thousand moons shall wane

A man upon a stall may find,
    And, passing, turn the page that tells
    A grief, then changed to something else
Sung by a long-forgotten mind.

But what of that? My darken'd ways
    Shall ring with music all the same;
    To breathe my loss is more than fame,
To utter love more sweet than praise.

LXXVIII

Again at Christmas did we weave
    The holly round the Christmas hearth;
    The silent snow possess'd the earth,
And calmly fell our Christmas-eve:

The yule-clog sparkled keen with frost,
    No wing of wind the region swept,
    But over all things brooding slept
The quiet sense of something lost.

As in the winters left behind,
    Again our ancient games had place,
    The mimic picture's breathing grace,
And dance and song and hoodman-blind.

Who show'd a token of distress?
    No single tear, no mark of pain:
    O sorrow, then can sorrow wane?
O grief, can grief be changed to less?

O last regret, regret can die!
 No—mixt with all this mystic frame.
 Her deep relations are the same,
But with long use her tears are dry.

LXXIX

'More than my brothers are to me,'—
    Let this not vex thee, noble heart!
    I know thee of what force thou art
To hold the costliest love in fee.

But thou and I are one in kind,
    As moulded like in Nature's mint;
    And hill and wood and field did print
The same sweet forms in either mind.

For us the same cold streamlet curl'd
    Thro' all his eddying coves; the same
    All winds that roam the twilight came
In whispers of the beauteous world.

At one dear knee we proffer'd vows,
    One lesson from one book we learn'd,
    Ere childhood's flaxen ringlet turn'd
To black and brown on kindred brows.

And so my wealth resembles thine,
    But he was rich where I was poor,
    And he supplied my want the more
As his unlikeness fitted mine.

LXXX

If any vague desire should rise,
    That holy Death ere Arthur died
    Had moved me kindly from his side,
    And dropt the dust on tearless eyes;

Then fancy shapes, as fancy can,
    The grief my loss in him had wrought,
    A grief as deep as life or thought,
But stay'd in peace with God and man.

I make a picture in the brain;
    I hear the sentence that he speaks;
    He bears the burthen of the weeks
But turns his burthen into gain.

His credit thus shall set me free;
    And, influence-rich to soothe and save,
    Unused example from the grave
Reach out dead hands to comfort me.

LXXXI

Could I have said while he was here,
   'My love shall now no further range;
   There cannot come a mellower change,
For now is love mature in ear.'

Love, then, had hope of richer store:
   What end is here to my complaint?
   This haunting whisper makes me faint,
'More years had made me love thee more.'

But Death returns an answer sweet:
   'My sudden frost was sudden gain,
   And gave all ripeness to the grain,
It might have drawn from after-heat.'

LXXXII

I wage not any feud with Death
    For changes wrought on form and face;
    No lower life that earth's embrace
May breed with him, can fright my faith.

Eternal process moving on,
    From state to state the spirit walks;
    And these are but the shatter'd stalks,
Or ruin'd chrysalis of one.

Nor blame I Death, because he bare
    The use of virtue out of earth:
    I know transplanted human worth
Will bloom to profit, otherwhere.

For this alone on Death I wreak
    The wrath that garners in my heart;
    He put our lives so far apart
We cannot hear each other speak.

LXXIII

Dip down upon the northern shore,
   O sweet new-year delaying long;
   Thou doest expectant nature wrong;
Delaying long, delay no more.

What stays thee from the clouded noons,
   Thy sweetness from its proper place?
   Can trouble live with April days,
Or sadness in the summer moons?

Bring orchis, bring the foxglove spire,
   The little speedwell's darling blue,
   Deep tulips dash'd with fiery dew,
Laburnums, dropping-wells of fire.

O thou, new-year, delaying long,
   Delayest the sorrow in my blood,
   That longs to burst a frozen bud
And flood a fresher throat with song.

LXXXIV

When I contemplate all alone
    The life that had been thine below,
    And fix my thoughts on all the glow
To which thy crescent would have grown;

I see thee sitting crown'd with good,
    A central warmth diffusing bliss
    In glance and smile, and clasp and kiss,
On all the branches of thy blood;

Thy blood, my friend, and partly mine;
    For now the day was drawing on,
    When thou should'st link thy life with one
Of mine own house, and boys of thine

Had babbled 'Uncle' on my knee;
    But that remorseless iron hour
    Made cypress of her orange flower,
Despair of Hope, and earth of thee.

I seem to meet their least desire,
    To clap their cheeks, to call them mine.
    I see their unborn faces shine
Beside the never-lighted fire.

I see myself an honor'd guest,
    Thy partner in the flowery walk
    Of letters, genial table-talk,
Or deep dispute, and graceful jest;

While now thy prosperous labor fills
    The lips of men with honest praise,
    And sun by sun the happy days
Descend below the golden hills

With promise of a morn as fair;
    And all the train of bounteous hours
    Conduct by paths of growing powers,
To reverence and the silver hair;

Till slowly worn her earthly robe,
    Her lavish mission richly wrought,

Leaving great legacies of thought,
Thy spirit should fail from off the globe;

What time mine own might also flee,
    As link'd with thine in love and fate,
    And, hovering o'er the dolorous strait
To the other shore, involved in thee,

Arrive at last the blessed goal,
    And He that died in Holy Land
    Would reach us out the shining hand,
And take us as a single soul.

What reed was that on which I leant?
    Ah, backward fancy, wherefore wake
    The old bitterness again, and break
The low beginnings of content.

LXXXV

This truth came borne with bier and pall,
   I felt it, when I sorrow'd most,
   'Tis better to have loved and lost,
Than never to have loved at all—

O true in word, and tried in deed,
   Demanding, so to bring relief
   To this which is our common grief,
What kind of life is that I lead;

And whether trust in things above
   Be dimm'd of sorrow, or sustain'd;
   And whether love for him have drain'd
My capabilities of love;

Your words have virtue such as draws
   A faithful answer from the breast,
   Thro' light reproaches, half exprest,
And loyal unto kindly laws.

My blood an even tenor kept,
    Till on mine ear this message falls,
    That in Vienna's fatal walls
God's finger touch'd him, and he slept.

The great Intelligences fair
    That range above our mortal state,
    In circle round the blessed gate,
Received and gave him welcome there;

And led him thro' the blissful climes,
    And show'd him in the fountain fresh
    All knowledge that the sons of flesh
Shall gather in the cycled times.

But I remain'd, whose hopes were dim,
    Whose life, whose thoughts were little worth,
    To wander on a darken'd earth,
Where all things round me breathed of him.

O friendship, equal-poised control,
    O heart, with kindliest motion warm,

O sacred essence, other form,
O solemn ghost, O crowned soul!

Yet none could better know than I,
   How much of act at human hands
   The sense of human will demands
By which we dare to live or die.

Whatever way my days decline,
   I felt and feel, tho' left alone,
   His being working in mine own,
The footsteps of his life in mine;

A life that all the Muses deck'd
   With gifts of grace, that might express
   All-comprehensive tenderness,
All-subtilising intellect:

And so my passion hath not swerved
   To works of weakness, but I find
   An image comforting the mind,
And in my grief a strength reserved.

Likewise the imaginative woe,

    That loved to handle spiritual strife

    Diffused the shock thro' all my life,

But in the present broke the blow.

My pulses therefore beat again

    For other friends that once I met;

    Nor can it suit me to forget

The mighty hopes that make us men.

I woo your love: I count it crime

    To mourn for any overmuch;

    I, the divided half of such

A friendship as had master'd Time;

Which masters Time indeed, and is

    Eternal, separate from fears:

    The all-assuming months and years

Can take no part away from this:

But Summer on the steaming floods,

    And Spring that swells the narrow brooks,

And Autumn, with a noise of rooks,
That gather in the waning woods,

And every pulse of wind and wave
    Recalls, in change of light or gloom,
    My old affection of the tomb,
And my prime passion in the grave:

My old affection of the tomb,
    A part of stillness, yearns to speak:
    'Arise, and get thee forth and seek
A friendship for the years to come.

'I watch thee from the quiet shore;
    Thy spirit up to mine can reach;
    But in dear words of human speech
We two communicate no more.'

And I, 'Can clouds of nature stain
    The starry clearness of the free?
    How is it? Canst thou feel for me
Some painless sympathy with pain?'

And lightly does the whisper fall:
> 'Tis hard for thee to fathom this;
> I triumph in conclusive bliss,
>
> And that serene result of all.'

So hold I commerce with the dead;
> Or so methinks the dead would say;
> Or so shall grief with symbols play
>
> And pining life be fancy-fed.

Now looking to some settled end,
> That these things pass, and I shall prove
> A meeting somewhere, love with love,
>
> I crave your pardon, O my friend;

If not so fresh, with love as true,
> I, clasping brother-hands, aver
> I could not, if I would, transfer
>
> The whole I felt for him to you.

For which be they that hold apart
> The promise of the golden hours?

First love, first friendship, equal powers,
That marry with the virgin heart.

Still mine, that cannot but deplore,
    That beats within a lonely place,
    That yet remembers his embrace,
But at his footstep leaps no more,

My heart, tho' widow'd, may not rest
    Quite in the love of what is gone,
    But seeks to beat in time with one
That warms another living breast.

Ah, take the imperfect gift I bring,
    Knowing the primrose yet is dear,
    The primrose of the later year,
As not unlike to that of Spring.

LXXXVI

Sweet after showers, ambrosial air,
    That rollest from the gorgeous gloom
    Of evening over brake and bloom
And meadow, slowly breathing bare

The round of space, and rapt below
    Thro' all the dewy-tassell'd wood,
    And shadowing down the horned flood
In ripples, fan my brows and blow

The fever from my cheek, and sigh
    The full new life that feeds thy breath
    Throughout my frame, till Doubt and Death,
Ill brethren, let the fancy fly

From belt to belt of crimson seas
    On leagues of odour streaming far,
    To where in yonder orient star
A hundred spirits whisper 'Peace.'

LXXXVII

I past beside the reverend walls
    In which of old I wore the gown;
    I roved at random thro' the town,
And saw the tumult of the halls;

And heard once more in college fanes
    The storm their high-built organs make,
    And thunder-music, rolling, shake
The prophet blazon'd on the panes;

And caught once more the distant shout,
    The measured pulse of racing oars
    Among the willows; paced the shores
And many a bridge, and all about

The same gray flats again, and felt
    The same, but not the same; and last
    Up that long walk of limes I past
To see the rooms in which he dwelt.

Another name was on the door:
    I linger'd; all within was noise
    Of songs, and clapping hands, and boys
That crash'd the glass and beat the floor;

Where once we held debate, a band
    Of youthful friends, on mind and art,
    And labour, and the changing mart,
And all the framework of the land;

When one would aim an arrow fair,
    But send it slackly from the string;
    And one would pierce an outer ring,
And one an inner, here and there;

And last the master-bowman, he,
    Would cleave the mark. A willing ear
    We lent him. Who, but hung to hear
The rapt oration flowing free

From point to point, with power and grace
    And music in the bounds of law,

To those conclusions when we saw
The God within him light his face,

And seem to lift the form, and glow
　In azure orbits heavenly-wise;
　And over those ethereal eyes
The bar of Michael Angelo?

LXXXVIII

Wild bird, whose warble, liquid sweet,
    Rings Eden thro' the budded quicks,
    O tell me where the senses mix,
O tell me where the passions meet,

Whence radiate: fierce extremes employ
    Thy spirits in the darkening leaf,
    And in the midmost heart of grief
Thy passion clasps a secret joy:

And I—my harp would prelude woe—
    I cannot all command the strings;
    The glory of the sum of things
Will flash along the chords and go.

LXXXIX

Witch-elms that counterchange the floor
    Of this flat lawn with dusk and bright;
    And thou, with all thy breadth and height
Of foliage, towering sycamore;

How often, hither wandering down,
    My Arthur found your shadows fair,
    And shook to all the liberal air
The dust and din and steam of town:

He brought an eye for all he saw;
    He mixt in all our simple sports;
    They pleased him, fresh from brawling courts
And dusty purlieus of the law.

O joy to him in this retreat,
    Inmantled in ambrosial dark,
    To drink the cooler air, and mark
The landscape winking thro' the heat:

O sound to rout the brood of cares,
    The sweep of scythe in morning dew,
    The gust that round the garden flew,
And tumbled half the mellowing pears!

O bliss, when all in circle drawn
    About him, heart and ear were fed
    To hear him, as he lay and read
The Tuscan poets on the lawn:

Or in the all-golden afternoon
    A guest, or happy sister, sung,
    Or here she brought the harp and flung
A ballad to the brightening moon:

Nor less it pleased in livelier moods,
    Beyond the bounding hill to stray,
    And break the livelong summer day
With banquet in the distant woods;

Whereat we glanced from theme to theme,
    Discuss'd the books to love or hate,

    Or touch'd the changes of the state,
Or threaded some Socratic dream;

But if I praised the busy town,
    He loved to rail against it still,
    For 'ground in yonder social mill
We rub each other's angles down,

'And merge,' he said, 'in form and gloss
    The picturesque of man and man.'
    We talk'd: the stream beneath us ran,
The wine-flask lying couch'd in moss,

Or cool'd within the glooming wave;
    And last, returning from afar,
    Before the crimson-circled star
Had fall'n into her father's grave,

And brushing ankle-deep in flowers,
    We heard behind the woodbine veil
    The milk that bubbled in the pail,
And buzzings of the honied hours.

XC

He tasted love with half his mind,
    Nor ever drank the inviolate spring
    Where nighest heaven, who first could fling
This bitter seed among mankind;

That could the dead, whose dying eyes
    Were closed with wail, resume their life,
    They would but find in child and wife
An iron welcome when they rise:

'Twas well, indeed, when warm with wine,
    To pledge them with a kindly tear,
    To talk them o'er, to wish them here,
To count their memories half divine;

But if they came who past away,
    Behold their brides in other hands;
    The hard heir strides about their lands,
And will not yield them for a day.

Yea, tho' their sons were none of these,
> Not less the yet-loved sire would make
> Confusion worse than death, and shake
The pillars of domestic peace.

Ah dear, but come thou back to me:
> Whatever change the years have wrought,
> I find not yet one lonely thought
That cries against my wish for thee.

XCI

When rosy plumelets tuft the larch,
   And rarely pipes the mounted thrush;
   Or underneath the barren bush
Flits by the sea-blue bird of March;

Come, wear the form by which I know
   Thy spirit in time among thy peers;
   The hope of unaccomplish'd years
Be large and lucid round thy brow.

When summer's hourly-mellowing change
   May breathe, with many roses sweet,
   Upon the thousand waves of wheat,
That ripple round the lonely grange;

Come: not in watches of the night,
   But where the sunbeam broodeth warm,
   Come, beauteous in thine after form,
And like a finer light in light.

XCII

If any vision should reveal
    Thy likeness, I might count it vain
    As but the canker of the brain;
Yea, tho' it spake and made appeal

To chances where our lots were cast
    Together in the days behind,
    I might but say, I hear a wind
Of memory murmuring the past.

Yea, tho' it spake and bared to view
    A fact within the coming year;
    And tho' the months, revolving near,
Should prove the phantom-warning true,

They might not seem thy prophecies,
    But spiritual presentiments,
    And such refraction of events
As often rises ere they rise.

XCIII

I shall not see thee. Dare I say
   No spirit ever brake the band
   That stays him from the native land
Where first he walk'd when claspt in clay?

No visual shade of some one lost,
   But he, the Spirit himself, may come
   Where all the nerve of sense is numb;
Spirit to Spirit, Ghost to Ghost.

O, therefore from thy sightless range
   With gods in unconjectured bliss,
   O, from the distance of the abyss
Of tenfold-complicated change,

Descend, and touch, and enter; hear
   The wish too strong for words to name;
   That in this blindness of the frame
My Ghost may feel that thine is near.

XCIV

How pure at heart and sound in head,
    With what divine affections bold
    Should be the man whose thought would hold
An hour's communion with the dead.

In vain shalt thou, or any, call
    The spirits from their golden day,
    Except, like them, thou too canst say,
My spirit is at peace with all.

They haunt the silence of the breast,
    Imaginations calm and fair,
    The memory like a cloudless air,
The conscience as a sea at rest:

But when the heart is full of din,
    And doubt beside the portal waits,
    They can but listen at the gates,
And hear the household jar within.

XCV

By night we linger'd on the lawn,
    For underfoot the herb was dry;
    And genial warmth; and o'er the sky
The silvery haze of summer drawn;

And calm that let the tapers burn
    Unwavering: not a cricket chirr'd:
    The brook alone far-off was heard,
And on the board the fluttering urn:

And bats went round in fragrant skies,
    And wheel'd or lit the filmy shapes
    That haunt the dusk, with ermine capes
And woolly breasts and beaded eyes;

While now we sang old songs that peal'd
    From knoll to knoll, where, couch'd at ease,
    The white kine glimmer'd, and the trees
Laid their dark arms about the field.

But when those others, one by one,
    Withdrew themselves from me and night,
    And in the house light after light
Went out, and I was all alone,

A hunger seized my heart; I read
    Of that glad year which once had been,
    In those fall'n leaves which kept their green,
The noble letters of the dead:

And strangely on the silence broke
    The silent-speaking words, and strange
    Was love's dumb cry defying change
To test his worth; and strangely spoke

The faith, the vigour, bold to dwell
    On doubts that drive the coward back,
    And keen thro' wordy snares to track
Suggestion to her inmost cell.

So word by word, and line by line,
    The dead man touch'd me from the past,

And all at once it seem'd at last
The living soul was flash'd on mine,

And mine in his was wound, and whirl'd
About empyreal heights of thought,
And came on that which is, and caught
The deep pulsations of the world,

Aeonian music measuring out
The steps of Time—the shocks of Chance—
The blows of Death. At length my trance
Was cancell'd, stricken thro' with doubt.

Vague words! but ah, how hard to frame
In matter-moulded forms of speech,
Or ev'n for intellect to reach
Thro' memory that which I became:

Till now the doubtful dusk reveal'd
The knolls once more where, couch'd at ease,
The white kine glimmer'd, and the trees
Laid their dark arms about the field :

And suck'd from out the distant gloom
    A breeze began to tremble o'er
    The large leaves of the sycamore,
And fluctuate all the still perfume,

And gathering freshlier overhead,
    Rock'd the full-foliaged elms, and swung
    The heavy-folded rose, and flung
The lilies to and fro, and said,

'The dawn, the dawn,' and died away;
    And East and West, without a breath,
    Mixt their dim lights, like life and death,
To broaden into boundless day.

XCVI

You say, but with no touch of scorn,
    Sweet-hearted, you, whose light-blue eyes
    Are tender over drowning flies,
You tell me, doubt is Devil-born.

I know not: one indeed I knew
    In many a subtle question versed,
    Who touch'd a jarring lyre at first,
But ever strove to make it true:

Perplext in faith, but pure in deeds,
    At last he beat his music out.
    There lives more faith in honest doubt,
Believe me, than in half the creeds.

He fought his doubts and gather'd strength,
    He would not make his judgment blind,
    He faced the spectres of the mind
And laid them: thus he came at length

To find a stronger faith his own;
    And Power was with him in the night,
    Which makes the darkness and the light,
And dwells not in the light alone,

But in the darkness and the cloud,
    As over Sinaï's peaks of old,
    While Israel made their gods of gold,
Altho' the trumpet blew so loud.

XCVII

My love has talk'd with rocks and trees;
    He finds on misty mountain-ground
    His own vast shadow glory-crown'd;
He sees himself in all he sees.

Two partners of a married life—
    I look'd on these and thought of thee
    In vastness and in mystery,
And of my spirit as of a wife.

These two—they dwelt with eye on eye,
    Their hearts of old have beat in tune,
    Their meetings made December June
Their every parting was to die.

Their love has never pastaway;
    The days she never can forget
    Are earnest that he loves her yet,
Whate'er the faithless people say.

Her life is lone, he sits apart,
    He loves her yet, she will not weep,
    Tho' rapt in matters dark and deep
He seems to slight her simple heart.

He thrids the labyrinth of the mind,
    He reads the secret of the star,
    He seems so near and yet so far,
He looks so cold: she thinks him kind.

She keeps the gift of years before,
    A wither'd violet is her bliss:
    She knows not what his greatness is,
For that, for all, she loves him more.

For him she plays, to him she sings
    Of early faith and plighted vows;
    She knows but matters of the house,
And he, he knows a thousand things.

Her faith is fixt and cannot move,
    She darkly feels him great and wise,

She dwells on him with faithful eyes,
'I cannot understand: I love.'

XCVIII

You leave us: you will see the Rhine,
    And those fair hills I sail'd below,
    When I was there with him; and go
By summer belts of wheat and vine

To where he breathed his latest breath,
    That City. All her splendour seems
    No livelier than the wisp that gleams
On Lethe in the eyes of Death.

Let her great Danube rolling fair
    Enwind her isles, unmark'd of me:
    I have not seen, I will not see
Vienna; rather dream that there,

A treble darkness, Evil haunts
    The birth, the bridal; friend from friend
    Is oftener parted, fathers bend
Above more graves, a thousand wants

Gnarr at the heels of men, and prey
    By each cold hearth, and sadness flings
    Her shadow on the blaze of kings:
And yet myself have heard him say,

That not in any mother town
    With statelier progress to and fro
    The double tides of chariots flow
By park and suburb under brown

Of lustier leaves; nor more content,
    He told me, lives in any crowd,
    When all is gay with lamps, and loud
With sport and song, in booth and tent,

Imperial halls, or open plain;
    And wheels the circled dance, and breaks
    The rocket molten into flakes
Of crimson or in emerald rain.

XCIX

Risest thou thus, dim dawn, again,
    So loud with voices of the birds,
    So thick with lowings of the herds,
Day, when I lost the flower of men;

Who tremblest thro' thy darkling red
    On yon swoll'n brook that bubbles fast
    By meadows breathing of the past,
And woodlands holy to the dead;

Who murmurest in the foliaged eaves
    A song that slights the coming care,
    And Autumn laying here and there
A fiery finger on the leaves;

Who wakenest with thy balmy breath
    To myriads on the genial earth,
    Memories of bridal, or of birth,
And unto myriads more, of death.

O, wheresoever those may be,
    Betwixt the slumber of the poles,
    To-day they count as kindred souls;
They know me not, but mourn with me.

C

I climb the hill: from end to end
    Of all the landscape underneath,
    I find no place that does not breathe
Some gracious memory of my friend;

No gray old grange, or lonely fold,
    Or low morass and whispering reed,
    Or simple stile from mead to mead,
Or sheepwalk up the windy wold;

Nor hoary knoll of ash and haw
    That hears the latest linnet trill,
    Nor quarry trench'd along the hill
And haunted by the wrangling daw;

Nor runlet tinkling from the rock;
    Nor pastoral rivulet that swerves
    To left and right thro' meadowy curves,
That feed the mothers of the flock;

But each has pleased a kindred eye,
    And each reflects a kindlier day;
    And, leaving these, to pass away,
I think once more he seems to die.

CI

Unwatch'd, the garden bough shall sway,
    The tender blossom flutter down,
    Unloved, that beech will gather brown,
This maple burn itself away;

Unloved, the sun-flower, shining fair,
    Ray round with flames her disk of seed,
    And many a rose carnation feed
With summer spice the humming air;

Unloved, by many a sandy bar,
    The brook shall babble down the plain,
    At noon or when the lesser wain
Is twisting round the polar star;

Uncared for, gird the windy grove,
    And flood the haunts of hern and crake;
    Or into silver arrows break
The sailing moon in creek and cove;

Till from the garden and the wild
    A fresh association blow,
    And year by year the landscape grow
Familiar to the stranger's child;

As year by year the labourer tills
    His wonted glebe, or lops the glades;
    And year by year our memory fades
From all the circle of the hills.

CII

We leave the well-beloved place
    Where first we gazed upon the sky;
    The roofs, that heard our earliest cry,
Will shelter one of stranger race.

We go, but ere we go from home,
    As down the garden-walks I move,
    Two spirits of a diverse love
Contend for loving masterdom.

One whispers, 'Here thy boyhood sung
    Long since its matin song, and heard
    The low love-language of the bird
In native hazels tassel-hung.'

The other answers, 'Yea, but here
    Thy feet have stray'd in after hours
    With thy lost friend among the bowers,
And this hath made them trebly dear.'

These two have striven half the day,
    And each prefers his separate claim,
    Poor rivals in a losing game,
That will not yield each other way.

I turn to go: my feet are set
    To leave the pleasant fields and farms;
    They mix in one another's arms
To one pure image of regret.

CIII

On that last night before we went
    From out the doors where I was bred,
    I dream'd a vision of the dead,
Which left my after-morn content.

Methought I dwelt within a hall,
    And maidens with me: distant hills
    From hidden summits fed with rills
A river sliding by the wall.

The hall with harp and carol rang.
    They sang of what is wise and good
    And graceful. In the centre stood
A statue veil'd, to which they sang;

And which, tho' veil'd, was known to me,
    The shape of him I loved, and love
    For ever: then flew in a dove
And brought a summons from the sea:

And when they learnt that I must go
>   They wept and wail'd, but led the way
>   To where a little shallop lay
At anchor in the flood below;

And on by many a level mead,
>   And shadowing bluff that made the banks,
>   We glided winding under ranks
Of iris, and the golden reed;

And still as vaster grew the shore
>   And roll'd the floods in grander space,
>   The maidens gather'd strength and grace
And presence, lordlier than before;

And I myself, who sat apart
>   And watch'd them, wax'd in every limb;
>   I felt the thews of Anakim,
The pulses of a Titan's heart;

As one would sing the death of war,
>   And one would chant the history

Of that great race, which is to be,
And one the shaping of a star;

Until the forward-creeping tides
  Began to foam, and we to draw
  From deep to deep, to where we saw
A great ship lift her shining sides.

The man we loved was there on deck,
  But thrice as large as man he bent
  To greet us. Up the side I went,
And fell in silence on his neck;

Whereat those maidens with one mind
  Bewail'd their lot; I did them wrong:
  'We served thee here,' they said, 'so long,
And wilt thou leave us now behind?'

So rapt I was, they could not win
  An answer from my lips, but he
  Replying, 'Enter likewise ye
And go with us:' they enter'd in.

And while the wind began to sweep
    A music out of sheet and shroud,
    We steer'd her toward a crimson cloud
That landlike slept along the deep.

CIV

The time draws near the birth of Christ;
    The moon is hid, the night is still;
    A single church below the hill
Is pealing, folded in the mist.

A single peal of bells below,
    That wakens at this hour of rest
    A single murmur in the breast,
That these are not the bells I know.

Like strangers' voices here they sound,
    In lands where not a memory strays,
    Nor landmark breathes of other days,
But all is new unhallow'd ground.

CV

To-night ungather'd let us leave
    This laurel, let this holly stand:
    We live within the stranger's land,
And strangely falls our Christmas-eve.

Our father's dust is left alone
    And silent under other snows:
    There in due time the woodbine blows,
The violet comes, but we are gone.

No more shall wayward grief abuse
    The genial hour with mask and mime,
    For change of place, like growth of time,
Has broke the bond of dying use.

Let cares that petty shadows cast,
    By which our lives are chiefly proved,
    A little spare the night I loved,
And hold it solemn to the past.

But let no footstep beat the floor,

    Nor bowl of wassail mantle warm;

    For who would keep an ancient form

Thro' which the spirit breathes no more?

Be neither song, nor game, nor feast;

    Nor harp be touch'd, nor flute be blown;

    No dance, no motion, save alone

What lightens in the lucid east

Of rising worlds by yonder wood.

    Long sleeps the summer in the seed;

    Run out your measured arcs, and lead

The closing cycle rich in good.

CVI

Ring out, wild bells, to the wild sky,
    The flying cloud, the frosty light:
    The year is dying in the night;
Ring out, wild bells, and let him die.

Ring out the old, ring in the new,
    Ring, happy bells, across the snow:
    The year is going, let him go;
Ring out the false, ring in the true.

Ring out the grief that saps the mind,
    For those that here we see no more;
    Ring out the feud of rich and poor,
Ring in redress to all mankind.

Ring out a slowly dying cause,
    And ancient forms of party strife;
    Ring in the nobler modes of life,
With sweeter manners, purer laws.

Ring out the want, the care, the sin,
    The faithless coldness of the times;
    Ring out, ring out my mournful rhymes,
But ring the fuller minstrel in.

Ring out false pride in place and blood,
    The civic slander and the spite;
    Ring in the love of truth and right,
Ring in the common love of good.

Ring out old shapes of foul disease;
    Ring out the narrowing lust of gold;
    Ring out the thousand wars of old,
Ring in the thousand years of peace.

Ring in the valiant man and free,
    The larger heart, the kindlier hand;
    Ring out the darkness of the land,
Ring in the Christ that is to be.

CVII

It is the day when he was born,
    A bitter day that early sank
    Behind a purple-frosty bank
Of vapour, leaving night forlorn.

The time admits not flowers or leaves
    To deck the banquet. Fiercely flies
    The blast of North and East, and ice
Makes daggers at the sharpen'd eaves,

And bristles all the brakes and thorns
    To yon hard crescent, as she hangs
    Above the wood which grides and clangs
Its leafless ribs and iron horns

Together, in the drifts that pass
    To darken on the rolling brine
    That breaks the coast. But fetch the wine,
Arrange the board and brim the glass;

Bring in great logs and let them lie,
    To make a solid core of heat;
    Be cheerful-minded, talk and treat
Of all things ev'n as he were by;

We keep the day. With festal cheer,
    With books and music, surely we
    Will drink to him, whate'er he be,
And sing the songs he loved to hear.

CVIII

I will not shut me from my kind,
    And, lest I stiffen into stone,
    I will not eat my heart alone,
Nor feed with sighs a passing wind:

What profit lies in barren faith,
    And vacant yearning, tho' with might
    To scale the heaven's highest height,
Or dive below the wells of Death?

What find I in the highest place,
    But mine own phantom chanting hymns?
    And on the depths of death there swims
The reflex of a human face.

I'll rather take what fruit may be
    Of sorrow under human skies:
    'Tis held that sorrow makes us wise,
Whatever wisdom sleep with thee.

CIX

Heart-affluence in discursive talk
   From household fountains never dry;
   The critic clearness of an eye,
That saw thro' all the Muses' walk;

Seraphic intellect and force
   To seize and throw the doubts of man;
   Impassion'd logic, which outran
The hearer in its fiery course;

High nature amorous of the good,
   But touch'd with no ascetic gloom;
   And passion pure in snowy bloom
Thro' all the years of April blood;

A love of freedom rarely felt,
   Of freedom in her regal seat
   Of England; not the schoolboy heat,
The blind hysterics of the Celt;

And manhood fused with female grace
    In such a sort, the child would twine
    A trustful hand, unask'd, in thine,
And find his comfort in thy face;

All these have been, and thee mine eyes
    Have look'd on: if they look'd in vain,
    My shame is greater who remain,
Nor let thy wisdom make me wise.

CX

Thy converse drew us with delight,
    The men of rathe and riper years:
    The feeble soul, a haunt of fears,
Forgot his weakness in thy sight.

On thee the loyal-hearted hung,
    The proud was half disarm'd of pride,
    Nor cared the serpent at thy side
To flicker with his double tongue.

The stern were mild when thou wert by,
    The flippant put himself to school
    And heard thee, and the brazen fool
Was soften'd, and he knew not why;

While I, thy nearest, sat apart,
    And felt thy triumph was as mine;
    And loved them more, that they were thine,
The graceful tact, the Christian art;

Nor mine the sweetness or the skill,
    But mine the love that will not tire,
    And, born of love, the vague desire
That spurs an imitative will.

CXI

The churl in spirit, up or down
    Along the scale of ranks, thro' all,
    To him who grasps a golden ball,
By blood a king, at heart a clown;

The churl in spirit, howe'er he veil
    His want in forms for fashion's sake,
    Will let his coltish nature break
At seasons thro' the gilded pale:

For who can always act? but he,
    To whom a thousand memories call,
    Not being less but more than all
The gentleness he seem'd to be,

Best seem'd the thing he was, and join'd
    Each office of the social hour
    To noble manners, as the flower
And native growth of noble mind;

Nor ever narrowness or spite,
    Or villain fancy fleeting by,
    Drew in the expression of an eye,
Where God and Nature met in light;

And thus he bore without abuse
    The grand old name of gentleman,
    Defamed by every charlatan,
And soil'd with all ignoble use.

CXII

High wisdom holds my wisdom less,
    That I, who gaze with temperate eyes
    On glorious insufficiencies,
Set light by narrower perfectness.

But thou, that fillest all the room
    Of all my love, art reason why
    I seem to cast a careless eye
On souls, the lesser lords of doom.

For what wert thou? some novel power
    Sprang up for ever at a touch,
    And hope could never hope too much,
In watching thee from hour to hour,

Large elements in order brought,
    And tracts of calm from tempest made,
    And world-wide fluctuation sway'd
In vassal tides that follow'd thought.

CXIII

'Tis held that sorrow makes us wise;
    Yet how much wisdom sleeps with thee
    Which not alone had guided me,
But served the seasons that may rise;

For can I doubt, who knew thee keen
    In intellect, with force and skill
    To strive, to fashion, to fulfil—
I doubt not what thou wouldst have been:

A life in civic action warm,
    A soul on highest mission sent,
    A potent voice of Parliament,
A pillar steadfast in the storm,

Should licensed boldness gather force,
    Becoming, when the time has birth,
    A lever to uplift the earth
And roll it in another course,

With thousand shocks that come and go,
    With agonies, with energies,
    With overthrowings, and with cries
And undulations to and fro.

CXIV

Who loves not Knowledge? Who shall rail
    Against her beauty? May she mix
    With men and prosper! Who shall fix
Her pillars? Let her work prevail.

But on her forehead sits a fire:
    She sets her forward countenance
    And leaps into the future chance,
Submitting all things to desire.

Half-grown as yet, a child, and vain—
    She cannot fight the fear of death.
    What is she, cut from love and faith,
But some wild Pallas from the brain

Of Demons? fiery-hot to burst
    All barriers in her onward race
    For power. Let her know her place;
She is the second, not the first.

A higher hand must make her mild,
    If all be not in vain; and guide
    Her footsteps, moving side by side
With wisdom, like the younger child:

For she is earthly of the mind,
    But Wisdom heavenly of the soul.
    O, friend, who camest to thy goal
So early, leaving me behind,

I would the great world grew like thee,
    Who grewest not alone in power
    And knowledge, but by year and hour
In reverence and in charity.

CXV

Now fades the last long streak of snow,
    Now burgeons every maze of quick
    About the flowering squares, and thick
By ashen roots the violets blow.

Now rings the woodland loud and long,
    The distance takes a lovelier hue,
    And drown'd in yonder living blue
The lark becomes a sightless song.

Now dance the lights on lawn and lea,
    The flocks are whiter down the vale,
    And milkier every milky sail
On winding stream or distant sea;

Where now the seamew pipes, or dives
    In yonder greening gleam, and fly
    The happy birds, that change their sky
To build and brood; that live their lives

From land to land; and in my breast
    Spring wakens too; and my regret
    Becomes an April violet,
And buds and blossoms like the rest.

CXVI

Is it, then, regret for buried time
    That keenlier in sweet April wakes,
    And meets the year, and gives and takes
The colours of the crescent prime?

Not all: the songs, the stirring air,
    The life re-orient out of dust
    Cry thro' the sense to hearten trust
In that which made the world so fair.

Not all regret: the face will shine
    Upon me, while I muse alone;
    And that dear voice, I once have known,
Still speak to me of me and mine:

Yet less of sorrow lives in me
    For days of happy commune dead;
    Less yearning for the friendship fled,
Than some strong bond which is to be.

CXVII

O days and hours, your work is this
   To hold me from my proper place,
   A little while from his embrace,
For fuller gain of after bliss:

That out of distance might ensue
   Desire of nearness doubly sweet;
   And unto meeting when we meet,
Delight a hundredfold accrue,

For every grain of sand that runs,
   And every span of shade that steals,
   And every kiss of toothed wheels,
And all the courses of the suns.

CXVIII

Contemplate all this work of Time,
    The giant labouring in his youth;
    Nor dream of human love and truth,
As dying Nature's earth and lime;

But trust that those we call the dead
    Are breathers of an ampler day
    For ever nobler ends. They say,
The solid earth whereon we tread

In tracts of fluent heat began,
    And grew to seeming-random forms,
    The seeming prey of cyclic storms,
Till at the last arose the man;

Who throve and branch'd from clime to clime,
    The herald of a higher race,
    And of himself in higher place,
If so he type this work of time

Within himself, from more to more;
    Or, crown'd with attributes of woe
    Like glories, move his course, and show
That life is not as idle ore,

But iron dug from central gloom,
    And heated hot with burning fears,
    And dipt in baths of hissing tears,
And batter'd with the shocks of doom

To shape and use. Arise and fly
    The reeling Faun, the sensual feast;
    Move upward, working out the beast,
And let the ape and tiger die.

CXIX

Doors, where my heart was used to beat
    So quickly, not as one that weeps
    I come once more; the city sleeps;
I smell the meadow in the street;

I hear a chirp of birds; I see
    Betwixt the black fronts long-withdrawn
    A light-blue lane of early dawn,
And think of early days and thee,

And bless thee, for thy lips are bland,
    And bright the friendship of thine eye;
    And in my thoughts with scarce a sigh
I take the pressure of thine hand.

CXX

I trust I have not wasted breath:
    I think we are not wholly brain,
    Magnetic mockeries; not in vain,
Like Paul with beasts, I fought with Death;

Not only cunning casts in clay:
    Let Science prove we are, and then
    What matters Science unto men,
At least to me? I would not stay.

Let him, the wiser man who springs
    Hereafter, up from childhood shape
    His action like the greater ape,
But I was *born* to other things.

CXXI

Sad Hesper o'er the buried sun
   And ready, thou, to die with him,
   Thou watchest all things ever dim
And dimmer, and a glory done:

The team is loosen'd from the wain,
   The boat is drawn upon the shore;
   Thou listenest to the closing door,
And life is darken'd in the brain.

Bright Phosphor, fresher for the night,
   By thee the world's great work is heard
   Beginning, and the wakeful bird;
Behind thee comes the greater light:

The market boat is on the stream,
   And voices hail it from the brink;
   Thou hear'st the village hammer clink,
And see'st the moving of the team.

Sweet Hesper-Phosphor, double name
    For what is one, the first, the last,
    Thou, like my present and my past,
Thy place is changed; thou art the same.

CXXII

Oh, wast thou with me, dearest, then,
    While I rose up against my doom,
    And yearn'd to burst the folded gloom,
To bare the eternal Heavens again,

To feel once more, in placid awe,
    The strong imagination roll
    A sphere of stars about my soul,
In all her motion one with law;

If thou wert with me, and the grave
    Divide us not, be with me now,
    And enter in at breast and brow,
Till all my blood, a fuller wave,

Be quicken'd with a livelier breath,
    And like an inconsiderate boy,
    As in the former flash of joy,
I slip the thoughts of life and death;

And all the breeze of Fancy blows,
    And every dew-drop paints a bow,
    The wizard lightnings deeply glow,
And every thought breaks out a rose.

CXXIII

There rolls the deep where grew the tree.
    O earth, what changes hast thou seen!
    There where the long street roars, hath been
The stillness of the central sea.

The hills are shadows, and they flow
    From form to form, and nothing stands;
    They melt like mist, the solid lands,
Like clouds they shape themselves and go.

But in my spirit will I dwell,
    And dream my dream, and hold it true;
    For tho' my lips may breathe adieu,
I cannot think the thing farewell.

CXXIV

That which we dare invoke to bless;
    Our dearest faith; our ghastliest doubt;
    He, They, One, All; within, without;
The Power in darkness whom we guess;

I found Him not in world or sun,
    Or eagle's wing, or insect's eye;
    Nor thro' the questions men may try,
The petty cobwebs we have spun:

If e'er when faith had fall'n asleep,
    I heard a voice 'believe no more'
    And heard an ever-breaking shore
That tumbled in the Godless deep;

A warmth within the breast would melt
    The freezing reason's colder part,
    And like a man in wrath the heart
Stood up and answer'd 'I have felt.'

No, like a child in doubt and fear:

    But that blind clamour made me wise;

    Then was I as a child that cries,

But, crying, knows his father near;

And what I am beheld again

    What is, and no man understands;

    And out of darkness came the hands

That reach thro' nature, moulding men.

CXXV

Whatever I have said or sung,
    Some bitter notes my harp would give,
    Yea, tho' there often seem'd to live
A contradiction on the tongue,

Yet Hope had never lost her youth;
    She did but look through dimmer eyes;
    Or Love but play'd with gracious lies,
Because he felt so fix'd in truth:

And if the song were full of care,
    He breathed the spirit of the song;
    And if the words were sweet and strong
He set his royal signet there;

Abiding with me till I sail
    To seek thee on the mystic deeps,
    And this electric force, that keeps
A thousand pulses dancing, fail.

CXXVI

Love is and was my Lord and King,
   And in his presence I attend
   To hear the tidings of my friend,
Which every hour his couriers bring.

Love is and was my King and Lord,
   And will be, tho' as yet I keep
   Within his court on earth, and sleep
Encompass'd by his faithful guard,

And hear at times a sentinel
   Who moves about from place to place,
   And whispers to the worlds of space,
In the deep night, that all is well.

CXXVII

And all is well, tho' faith and form
    Be sunder'd in the night of fear;
    Well roars the storm to those that hear
A deeper voice across the storm,

Proclaiming social truth shall spread,
    And justice, ev'n tho' thrice again
    The red fool-fury of the Seine
Should pile her barricades with dead.

But ill for him that wears a crown,
    And him, the lazar, in his rags:
    They tremble, the sustaining crags;
The spires of ice are toppled down,

And molten up, and roar in flood;
    The fortress crashes from on high,
    The brute earth lightens to the sky,
And the great Aeon sinks in blood,

And compass'd by the fires of Hell;
    While thou, dear spirit, happy star,
    O'erlook'st the tumult from afar,
And smilest, knowing all is well.

CXXVIII

The love that rose on stronger wings,
    Unpalsied when he met with Death,
    Is comrade of the lesser faith
That sees the course of human things.

No doubt vast eddies in the flood
    Of onward time shall yet be made,
    And throned races may degrade;
Yet, O ye mysteries of good,

Wild Hours that fly with Hope and Fear,
    If all your office had to do
    With old results that look like new;
If this were all your mission here,

To draw, to sheathe a useless sword,
    To fool the crowd with glorious lies,
    To cleave a creed in sects and cries,
To change the bearing of a word,

To shift an arbitrary power,
    To cramp the student at his desk,
    To make old bareness picturesque
And tuft with grass a feudal tower;

Why then my scorn might well descend
    On you and yours. I see in part
    That all, as in some piece of art,
Is toil coöperant to an end.

CXXIX

Dear friend, far off, my lost desire,
   So far, so near in woe and weal;
   O loved the most, when most I feel
There is a lower and a higher;

Known and unknown; human, divine;
   Sweet human hand and lips and eye;
   Dear heavenly friend that canst not die,
Mine, mine, for ever, ever mine;

Strange friend, past, present, and to be;
   Loved deeplier, darklier understood;
   Behold, I dream a dream of good,
And mingle all the world with thee.

CXXX

Thy voice is on the rolling air;
   I hear thee where the waters run;
   Thou standest in the rising sun,
And in the setting thou art fair.

What art thou then? I cannot guess;
   But tho' I seem in star and flower
   To feel thee some diffusive power,
I do not therefore love thee less:

My love involves the love before;
   My love is vaster passion now;
   Tho' mix'd with God and Nature thou,
I seem to love thee more and more.

Far off thou art, but ever nigh;
   I have thee still, and I rejoice;
   I prosper, circled with thy voice;
I shall not lose thee tho' I die.

CXXXI

O living will that shalt endure
    When all that seems shall suffer shock,
    Rise in the spiritual rock,
Flow thro' our deeds and make them pure,

That we may lift from out of dust
    A voice as unto him that hears,
    A cry above the conquer'd years
To one that with us works, and trust,

With faith that comes of self-control,
    The truths that never can be proved
    Until we close with all we loved,
And all we flow from, soul in soul.

EPILOGUE

O true and tried, so well and long,
    Demand not thoua marriage lay;
    In that it is thy marriage day
Is music more than any song.

Nor have I felt so much of bliss
    Since first he told me that he loved
    A daughter of our house; nor proved
Since that dark day a day like this;

Tho' I since then have number'd o'er
    Some thrice three years: they went and came,
    Remade the blood and changed the frame,
And yet is love not less, but more;

No longer caring to embalm
    In dying songs a dead regret,
    But like a statue solid-set,
And moulded in colossal calm.

Regret is dead, but love is more
    Than in the summers that are flown,
    For I myself with these have grown
To something greater than before;

Which makes appear the songs I made
    As echoes out of weaker times,
    As half but idle brawling rhymes,
The sport of random sun and shade.

But where is she, the bridal flower,
    That must be made a wife ere noon?
    She enters, glowing like the moon
Of Eden on its bridal bower:

On me she bends her blissful eyes
    And then on thee; they meet thy look
    And brighten like the star that shook
Betwixt the palms of paradise.

O when her life was yet in bud,
    He too foretold the perfect rose.

For thee she grew, for thee she grows
For ever, and as fair as good.

And thou art worthy; full of power;
    As gentle; liberal-minded, great,
    Consistent; wearing all that weight
Of learning lightly like a flower.

But now set out: the noon is near,
    And I must give away the bride;
    She fears not, or with thee beside
And me behind her, will not fear.

For I that danced her on my knee,
    That watch'd her on her nurse's arm,
    That shielded all her life from harm
At last must part with her to thee;

Now waiting to be made a wife,
    Her feet, my darling, on the dead
    Their pensive tablets round her head,
And the most living words of life

Breathed in her ear. The ring is on,
>   The 'wilt thou' answer'd, and again
>   The 'wilt thou' ask'd, till out of twain
Her sweet 'I will' has made you one.

Now sign your names, which shall be read,
>   Mute symbols of a joyful morn,
>   By village eyes as yet unborn;
The names are sign'd, and overhead

Begins the clash and clang that tells
>   The joy to every wandering breeze;
>   The blind wall rocks, and on the trees
The dead leaf trembles to the bells.

O happy hour, and happier hours
>   Await them. Many a merry face
>   Salutes them—maidens of the place,
That pelt us in the porch with flowers.

O happy hour, behold the bride
>   With him to whom her hand I gave.

They leave the porch, they pass the grave
That has to-day its sunny side.

To-day the grave is bright for me,
    For them the light of life increased,
    Who stay to share the morning feast,
Who rest to-night beside the sea.

Let all my genial spirits advance
    To meet and greet a whiter sun;
    My drooping memory will not shun
The foaming grape of eastern France.

It circles round, and fancy plays,
    And hearts are warm'd and faces bloom,
    As drinking health to bride and groom
We wish them store of happy days.

Nor count me all to blame if I
    Conjecture of a stiller guest,
    Perchance, perchance, among the rest,
And, tho' in silence, wishing joy.

But they must go, the time draws on,
    And those white-favour'd horses wait;
    They rise, but linger; it is late;
Farewell, we kiss, and they are gone.

A shade falls on us like the dark
    From little cloudlets on the grass,
    But sweeps away as out we pass
To range the woods, to roam the park,

Discussing how their courtship grew,
    And talk of others that are wed,
    And how she look'd, and what he said,
And back we come at fall of dew.

Again the feast, the speech, the glee,
    The shade of passing thought, the wealth
    Of words and wit, the double health,
The crowning cup, the three-times-three,

And last the dance;—till I retire:
    Dumb is that tower which spake so loud,

And high in heaven the streaming cloud,
And on the downs a rising fire:

And rise, O moon, from yonder down,
    Till over down and over dale
    All night the shining vapour sail
And pass the silent-lighted town,

The white-faced halls, the glancing rills,
    And catch at every mountain head,
    And o'er the friths that branch and spread
Their sleeping silver thro' the hills;

And touch with shade the bridal doors,
    With tender gloom the roof, the wall;
    And breaking let the splendour fall
To spangle all the happy shores

By which they rest, and ocean sounds,
    And, star and system rolling past,
    A soul shall draw from out the vast
And strike his being into bounds,

And, moved thro' life of lower phase,
    Result in man, be born and think,
    And act and love, a closer link
Betwixt us and the crowning race

Of those that, eye to eye, shall look
    On knowledge, under whose command
    Is Earth and Earth's, and in their hand
Is Nature like an open book;

No longer half-akin to brute,
    For all we thought and loved and did,
    And hoped, and suffer'd, is but seed
Of what in them is flower and fruit;

Whereof the man, that with me trod
    This planet, was a noble type
    Appearing ere the times were ripe,
That friend of mine who lives in God,

That God, which ever lives and loves,
    One God, one law, one element,

And one far-off divine event,
To which the whole creation moves.

译后记

1

这是一桩拖延太久的译事,我似乎已经忘了最初动心起念的缘由。也许,其中一个缘由是来自艾略特。在一篇谈论《悼念集》的文章里艾略特说:"如果没有技巧上的成熟,《悼念集》不会是一部伟大的诗作,丁尼生也不会是一个伟大的诗人。丁尼生是音韵大师,同时也是表现忧郁的大师;任何一位英语诗人都不曾拥有如他一般对元音极为灵敏的耳朵,以及对某些痛苦情绪精细入微的感受。……丁尼生所处的时代是一个已经具有强烈时间意识的时代:许多事情似乎正在发生,铁路正在兴建,新发现层出不穷,世界的面目正在改变。那是一个忙于与时俱进的时代。多数时候,它无法把握永恒的事物,无法把握有关人、上帝、生命以及死亡的永恒真理。外在的丁尼生随着他的时代而悸动;除了对语音独特而准确的感觉,他没有什么东西可以牢牢抓住。但在这方面他有任何人都不曾有的东西。外在的丁尼生,他在技巧上的成就,与他的内里紧密相连。……只有不带偏见地看待表层的东西,我们才最有可能进入内里深处,进入到深渊般的悲伤之中。丁尼生不只是一个二流的维吉尔,他与但丁眼中的维吉尔同在,一个身处幽灵之间的维吉尔,他是英国诗人中最为悲怆的一位,跻身于地狱之边的伟人之列。"

读到这段话时候的我,已深深懂得艾略特在说什么,关于诗人所承载的音韵、忧郁以及对于这二者精细的感受力,关于表层与深渊,关于变化、失去,以及带着怀疑接受一切变化和失去之后仍拥有的对于不变的信念。

关于一个在现代汉语新诗中未及完成就被轻易遗弃的浪漫主义诗学传统。

我希望借助翻译《悼念集》,就此做一点复活的尝试,正如丁尼生在写下这些诗篇时所做过的、复活友人的尝试。

2

《悼念集》正文部分共 131 首,外加后来补入的序曲和终曲,共 133 首,每首诗从最短的 12

行，到最长的144行，全部采用四行体、四音步抑扬格和abba的脚韵。很抱歉我没有能力完全遵从它的音律，但也没有完全舍弃。

在丁尼生之前，英诗最常见的音律是五音步抑扬格，若进一步落实到长诗和哀歌传统中，通行的韵脚则是abab。丁尼生从两方面打破了它。首先是从五音步到四音步，看似只是每行减少了两个音节，但造成的情感变化是强烈的，因为相对于五音步带来的听觉习惯上的完整感与信心感，四音步的每一行比期待的都更为短促，每一行似乎都是破碎、不完整和欲言又止的，每一行都在等待着下一行的拯救。而相对于abab韵脚的整饬，abba的韵脚安排，又带来一种迷离恍惚的回环感：每一段四行诗中第一行的a，仿佛一次次丧失在第二、三行陌生又漫长的b中，并一次次穿过这些漫长的陌生，奋力抵达第四行熟悉的a，又并非全然的回归，因为此刻第四行的a已然只是第一行a的微弱回声。如果说第一行的a指向过去，那么，在经历第二、三行b的镇定与盘旋之后，它所抵达的第四行的a却不在过去，而在未来。每一段四行诗，都是一场螺旋式的运动，携带着某种奇异的离心力，在将一切缠绕收紧的同时又将一切都散开，在分离的同时又保持为一个整体，让对于救赎和复活的信念伴随对此信念的怀疑同生共处。

在传统的哀歌主题中，要么是灵魂终于克服了悲哀，但曾经强烈的爱却也随之消失；要么，是自我征服了时间，遂听任自己耽溺在过去。《悼念集》与此二者都不相同，诗人最终克服了失去挚友的悲哀，但爱却依旧强烈而崭新；他征服了时间，却不仅仅活在拥有死者的过去，而是和死者一起生长，一起活在此刻所有的生命中，并期待在未知的更高处相遇。

在丁尼生这里，主题的创新与音律的创新，是一体的。abba 的抱韵虽然早在意大利体十四行诗中就有，但在十四行诗体中仅限于前两个诗节的八行，而丁尼生将此扩展到每一个诗节，并把五音步缩减为四音步，他希望用一种前所未有的形式，表达其所经受的无边无际的怆痛，以及随之而来的深沉又崭新的情感。因此，虽说在他之前，诸如本·琼生、锡德尼勋爵等诗人也曾偶尔用过此种音律，却丝毫不妨碍"悼念体"依旧成为英诗中最具独创性的诗体之一。

3

《悼念集》在 1850 年最初出版时的名字，是 IN MEMORIAM A.H.H.。这缩写字母的主人是亚瑟·亨利·哈勒姆，丁尼生青年时代的挚友。

哈勒姆是历史学家亨利·哈勒姆的儿子，出生于 1811 年 2 月，比丁尼生小十八个月。丁尼生 1827 年进入剑桥三一学院，第二年哈勒姆也来到这里，他们大约是在 1829 年春天相识的，迅速成为至交，又一起成为剑桥最具精英色彩的学术社团"使徒社"的一员。同年 12 月，丁尼生邀请哈勒姆前来萨默斯比的家中做客，在这里，哈勒姆爱上了丁尼生的妹妹——与他同龄的艾米莉，并私自订婚。这份意外的爱情加深了他们的友谊，同时也让哈勒姆的父亲大为光火。他禁止哈勒姆和艾米莉见面，但无法中断这份炽热的感情。1830 年夏天，丁尼生和哈勒姆去法国南部旅行。第二年，丁尼生的父亲，萨默斯比村的教区牧师乔治·丁尼生突然病逝，留下八个儿子和四个女儿，丁尼生虽非长子，此刻也毅然承担起责任，中断学业回到萨默斯比的家中，侍奉母亲和养育弟妹。1832 年 2 月，哈勒姆年满 21 岁之际，经过长久的坚持，他和丁尼生妹妹艾米莉的婚约得到了家庭的认可。随后，哈勒姆完成在剑桥的学业，赴伦敦学习法律，一切都朝着美满的方向发展。1833年夏天，哈勒姆和父亲计划去欧洲旅行，丁尼生去伦敦送别，这是他们最后一次见面。

1833年10月，丁尼生收到哈勒姆叔父的来信，信里告知哈勒姆因为突发脑溢血在维也纳病逝，遗体将通过船只从的雅里斯特海港运回英国安葬。此时哈勒姆年仅二十二岁。

对丁尼生而言，哈勒姆并非一个普通的好友，他是世上的光。丁尼生早年在寄宿学校生活时留下很深的阴影，进入剑桥之后也不如意，直到遇见哈勒姆。哈勒姆在剑桥享有极高的声誉，家世很好，才华超群，是一颗冉冉升起的明星。同时代人日后回忆他，公认他堪比当时最杰出的英国首相格莱斯顿，而格莱斯顿本人在晚年的回忆录里也对哈勒姆大加赞赏。可以想见，有这样一个杰出的同龄人作为知音，对丁尼生而言是多么大的鼓舞。哈勒姆鼓励丁尼生在1832年出版第一本个人诗集《抒情诗集》，并撰写长文《论现代诗歌的特征和丁尼生的抒情诗》，率先对友人的诗歌做出热诚而准确的高度评价。一个多世纪之后，对浪漫主义造诣甚深的美国批评家哈罗德·布鲁姆断言，迄今为止最好的关于丁尼生诗歌的论说，依旧还是来自哈勒姆。而在丁尼生经历父亲去世、兄弟生病、退学回家、诗集遭遇批评家酷评等诸多变故之际，来自哈勒姆的友谊也一直是他最坚定的慰藉和支撑。

就是这样一个难得一遇的卓绝的知己，他如此年轻和突然的死，必然让尚且苟活的那个人的生命也陷入黑暗。丁尼生对抗黑暗的方式，是写诗。

4

写诗，真的能够表达或疗愈悲哀吗？或者说，那些彻骨的无以名状的痛苦如何能够通过优雅美妙的修辞和韵律得以传达？在美和痛苦之间，在精巧的词语和混沌的感情之间，似乎总存在某种不可逾越的鸿沟，也因此，那些讲述痛苦的诗歌倘若越美丽，人们往往就越抱有疑虑。与丁尼生同时代的小说家夏洛蒂·勃朗特在读过《悼念集》初版后就写信给她的传记作者、小说家伊丽莎白·盖斯凯尔夫人，抱怨说读不下去整本诗集，她觉得这些诗是美丽的、悲哀的，却也是单调乏味的，她说，假如哈勒姆和丁尼生的关系确实非同一般，那么她就更加怀疑这些押韵的、字斟句酌的、印刷出来的纪念碑是否可以承载悲哀，因为那些真正深刻的悲哀应当随着时间加深，而无法仅仅表现为韵文。在这一点上，现代人显然会更亲近勃朗特，而非丁尼生。

然而，在写作这批诗的最初，丁尼生就已意识到会遭遇此种质疑，《悼念集》第5首可以视作对此的回答：

> 将自我感受的哀痛付诸文字，
> 　我有时以为这仿佛是一种罪愆，
> 　因为言语，犹如自然，半是呈现
> 半是将那内在的灵魂藏匿。

> 然而，对于永不安宁的头脑与心灵，
> 　字斟句酌的语言自有价值；
> 　那不足为道的技艺练习，
> 令痛苦麻木，似慢性毒品。

> 诗句，犹如黑纱，我用它裹住自己，
> 　犹如用粗陋麻衣抵御寒冷；
> 　　但那在词语包裹下的巨大哀痛
> 仍显出它的轮廓，且就如此而已。

哈勒姆的死，将一个以诗歌作为志业的人的写作从此割裂成两个部分，一部分是依旧面向公众的艺术创作，另一部分则是执着与死者交谈的任性私语。就在得知友人死讯后的一周内，丁尼生创作出他最伟大的诗篇之一，《尤利西斯》，随后又在几周内开启另一些著名长诗的写作计划，如《提托诺斯》和更为大型的历史叙事诗《亚瑟王之死》。这些诗的情感动机显然和哈勒姆有关，但那份私人情感被精心地隐藏在由某个神话人物所做出的戏剧性独白或有关某段历史传奇的戏剧性讲述中，仿佛只有戴着面具才能讲述有关悲伤的真理，只有进入另一些更为古老的有关他者的悲伤之中，才能将一己的悲伤予以缓解，并转化成某种普遍性的哀歌。这是独独属于诗人的工作。

然而这还不够。在真正深刻的悲哀面前，一个诗人投身于工作，充其量依旧只是一种自我疗愈的权宜之计，但丁尼生显然不满足于疗愈自我，他像一切失去至爱的伟大诗人一样，梦想的是复活那个被爱者。《悼念集》的写作就是一次关于复活的漫长尝试，这尝试与发表、出版无关，与打动他人无关，也与纪念碑无关，这尝试是一次走入地狱唤回至爱的绝望征程。因此，与丁尼生同期写作的其他诗歌不同，《悼念集》最初并不是一个有计划的整体性的写作，它只是不可遏制地在绝望与怀疑中奋力蔓延，生长，倘若它是一个整体，那也是如艾略特所言，"是一部日记式的整体，一部由一个男人的自白浓缩而成的日记。这是一部我们一个字都不能错过的日记"。

5

《悼念集》是日记，又不是日记。丁尼生自己曾如此回顾《悼念集》的写作："这是一部诗，而非一部实在的传记。它根基于我们的友谊，根基于哈勒姆和我妹妹艾米莉的婚约，根基于他在维也纳突然的死，根基于他在克利夫登教堂的葬礼。这部诗以我小妹妹塞西莉亚的婚礼颂歌作为结束，暗示某种类似但丁《神曲》一样的模式，即以幸福作为结束。这些诗分别写于不同时间和不同的地方，我起初并没有写组诗或出版的想法，直到我发现我已经写了很多。如同在戏剧中常见的那样，这些诗里不同阶段不同层次的悲哀情绪也具有某种戏剧性的设定感，我确信，唯有透过对于慈爱上帝的信念，人类种种的恐惧、怀疑和受难，才能找到答案，得以解除。而这些诗里的'我'，并非一个耽溺于谈论自己的作者本人，而是某种人类的声音在透过他说话。自哈勒姆的死算起，整组诗可以略微分成三个阶段，以哈勒姆死后的第一个圣诞节（第 28 首）、第二个圣诞节（第 78 首）和第三个圣诞节（第 104、105 首等）作为分界。"

可以说，《悼念集》的主体部分，基本在哈勒姆死后三年左右的时间就完成了，但随后，一直还有一些零星的诗章不断加入，就像一个人感觉似乎通过时间的帮助克服了伤痛，却依旧发觉生命阴晴不定。在哈勒姆死后的十年内，丁尼生抽烟酗酒，穷困潦倒，却从未停止写作，却也再未发表作品。直至 1842 年，他终于在朋友的鼓励劝说下出版了两卷本《诗集》，并大获成功。他继续暗自写作有关哈勒姆的哀歌，到了 1845 年，

《悼念集》已经接近现在的长度，但他一直推迟和延宕出版的进程。终于，1850年初，他开始自印了一个给小范围朋友看的没有名字的版本，又几经修改，在哈勒姆去世十七年后，1850年6月，《悼念集》正式出版，起印五千本，没有署名，题为 IN MEMORIAM A.H.H。同年9月诗集就再版，随后迅速成为现象级的畅销书。时人评论道，"语言和想象力的辉煌，思想和感情的深沉，形式的完美，在现代英诗中无出其右"。

《悼念集》深深地打动了维多利亚时代的人，丁尼生也因此荣膺新一任桂冠诗人。那个时代的英国人对于哀悼的传统无比熟悉，但《悼念集》中除了哀悼，还有一些更为崭新和诚实的情感，有关信仰与怀疑，进步与爱。

虽然达尔文的《进化论》比《悼念集》晚出版九年，但在达尔文之前，此类进化思想已蔚为大观，丁尼生比同时代诗人更关心科学发展，早就拜读过莱伊尔的《地质学原理》。莱伊尔认为，地球的变化一如人从儿童长至成人，不停变化，但没有事物会完全消失，他们只是进入下一个阶段。同样，《悼念集》中也有一个灵魂进化的模型，譬如在第43、44和45这几首诗中所描述的，尤其是第 45 首的末句：

> 倘若人们不得不重新自我学习，
> 在死所带来的第二次诞生之后。

这第二次诞生，是属于哈勒姆的，却也属于丁尼生本人。而第 47 首描述得更为明确，丁尼生想象那些在末日审判时复活的荣耀身体中仍能暂时保留个体性的灵魂，这种个体性的保留，依赖于灵魂在世时的卓越，这些卓越的灵魂将做最后一次相遇，随后，他们会失去各自的个性，并将各自的灵魂融入灵魂总体的海洋。丁尼生期待这最后的相遇，为此，他需要在此世保持最诚挚的善：

> 我们将在无尽的宴席中坐下，
> 　相互享受彼此的善：
> 　是什么样恢弘的梦能忍心刺伤
> 那在尘世属于爱神的柔情？至少
>
> 在最后的和最尖锐的高处，
> 　在我们的灵逐渐消散之前，

在靠岸处,他寻求一个拥抱和道别:

"珍重!我们把自我弃绝在光中。"

哈勒姆的灵魂激励着丁尼生,他想象哈勒姆存在于他的灵魂之中,用自己的理解力和智慧在帮助他,用其想象他人痛苦的能力:

> 同样地,那想象他人痛苦的能力,
> 　使我热爱从事精神性的斗争,
> 　并将那震惊贯穿我整个的生命,
> 但也随之缓解我当下的重创。

(第85首)

丁尼生信仰上帝却很少谈到教义,他坚持,"在诚实的怀疑中会升腾更强烈的信"(第96首),他和他的怀疑战斗,"一个全能者会创造一个充满痛苦的世界,这对我来讲某些时候是难以相信的",这种因为微弱个体的痛苦而产生的对于上帝的质疑,在陀思妥耶夫斯基的《宗教大法官》中,将得到更为深刻的阐发,但我们不要忘了,浪漫主义诗人丁尼生是和现实主义小说家陀思妥耶夫斯基同时代的人,是同样在怀疑和希望中奋力挣扎的十九世纪人。某种程度上，丁尼生《悼念集》所呈现的复杂情感，属于威廉·燕卜荪在《朦胧的七种类型》中所描述的第六种朦胧，即属于十九世纪诗歌特有的摇摆不定，"一方面，深思的状态既被渴求又被躲避；另一方面，'是一切，又什么都不是'的诗人，同时体验着生活的各个面"。

而支撑丁尼生的，除了对于灵魂进化的饱含理解力的推演，还有爱：

"我不能理解：我爱。"（第 97 首）

我并不拥有这些美妙与技艺，
　我只拥有那永不疲倦的爱，
　　以及一种源自爱的
鼓励我效仿你的朦胧热望。（第 110 首）

升腾自强力羽翼上的爱，
　不会在死亡面前瘫痪，
　　它是残存信仰的盟友
这信仰目睹人类向上的征程。

（第 128 首）

多年之后，经受了丧夫之痛的维多利亚女王对丁尼生说，"《悼念集》给予我的，是仅次于圣经的安慰"。

6

而哈罗德·布鲁姆的困惑在于，"为什么丁尼生在我们这个时代并未获得足够的声望，而和他相似却比他有限得多的马拉美却拥有之？"

我不知道这是否属于一个正当的困惑，因为这涉及是否同意布鲁姆对于马拉美的判断。但至少，相较于马拉美，丁尼生在当代汉语诗人中的确是毫无声望可言。这其中有许多原因暂且不论，我只希望这本《悼念集》的翻译，多多少少可以帮助促成一点改变。中西现代诗歌发展的不同步，百年时局的动荡，以及诸多有才华诗人的早逝，造成当代汉语新诗某种跑步进入现代主义的怪现状，以及随之而来的与世界潮流同步的幻觉。丁尼生当年拥抱进步，但他同样深知，所有进步，无论是社会还是艺术，其前提是对过往传统与习俗的一次次消化、吸收，一切都不曾消失，只是共同进入一个新阶段，而新事物的存在不必建立在一次次对于旧事物的打倒和捐弃上。

谢谢肖海鸥。她最初听我谈起丁尼生，就赠我诺顿批评版的《悼念集》，好些年后，这本译诗集却也最终奇妙地经由她手出版。也谢谢翁海贞，倘若不是她答应校对全部译稿，我几乎已经放弃了这件译事，而她认真细致地帮我指摘出无数词句翻译和理解上的硬伤，又赠我两本古旧版本的注疏，才使得我终于有勇气交出这份作业，并了却一桩心事。当然还要感谢飞白先生和黄杲炘先生，他们曾分别在《英国维多利亚时代诗选》（1985）和《丁尼生诗选》（1995）中，节译过《悼念集》的11首和36首，筚路蓝缕之功，实不可没。同时，也要感谢上海文艺出版社的余静双编辑，她在编辑拙译过程中又发现了很多错误，并写出详尽的修改意见，让我在惭愧之余，也再次体会到译事之艰难。

我在翻译之初，就期待能采取英汉双语文本的形式。一方面，这可以让读者更真切地感知丁尼生的音律之美，弥补在翻译中必然丧失之物；另一方面，也是对译者的鞭策与警醒。所有的翻译，如同所有的创作一样，很可能都是一种徒劳的努力，所以也非常期待读者诸君可以不吝赐教，以便日后有机会改进。

最后，我想私心附上一首十年前译的华兹华斯的长诗。因为正是译这首诗时的经验，让我得以更深刻地体会丁尼生当时的心境，也就此对浪漫主义诗歌有了全新的认知。从华兹华斯到丁尼生，是两代桂冠诗人的传承，却也是人类精神在面对一切困厄悲苦时不屈不挠的传承。就借这首诗最后的诗句作为结束语：

"感谢我们赖以生存的人类心灵，感谢它的温柔、欢乐与忧惧。"

张定浩

2020年1月24日，除夕于上海

附录

永生颂

威廉·华兹华斯

> 孩童是成人之父;
> 我愿那天然的敬爱
> 能贯穿我的一生。

1

犹记当年,草地、溪流还有果树,
这大地,以及每一样平常景象,
在我眼里似乎
都披着天光,
这荣耀,梦的开始。
只是现在已非从前;——
我环视四野,
白天黑夜,
再也见不到昔日之所见。

2

彩虹去了又来,

玫瑰依然可爱,

欢快的月亮

环视四周,天宇寥廓无蔽,

星夜的汪洋

散发着动人美丽;

初生的太阳辉煌灿烂;

但无论在哪里,我已明了

有一种荣耀已永离了人间。

3

如今,鸟雀们的欢唱依旧

羊羔们蹦跳依旧

像叮咚不停的手鼓,

唯独我,萌生一缕哀思:

及时的言说可以阻挡它的郁积,

于是我再次尝试坚强:

瀑布自悬崖吹起他们的号角;

我的哀思焉能再错失这季节的流光。

我听见回声在群山间流荡,

来自沉睡原野的风朝我呼啸,

大地一派欢欣;

地和海

在沉醉中放浪了形骸,

怀着五月之心,

每一头牲畜都置身节庆:——

你,欢乐之子,

在我身边呼喊吧,让我听你的喊声,你这幸福的牧羊少年。

4
你们有福的造物,我听见

你们彼此的呼唤;我看到

在你们的庆典上诸天也一同欢笑;

我的心融进你们的欢宴,

我的头顶自有它的花冠。

你们的幸福满盈,我有——我有全然的体验。

哦不幸的日子!倘若我愁苦

而大地正忙于装点,

这甜美的五月晨间,

孩子们正在摘选

鲜花;在四面八方,

在宽阔辽远的一千个山谷中;

阳光温暖,

婴儿欢腾在母亲的臂弯:——

我听见,我听见,我笑着听见!

—— 但是,众树中却有一树,

还有我曾打量过的孤独旷野,

他们一起诉说着,某些事物的殄灭:

三色堇在脚边

重复同样的流言:

那如幻的光辉逃到哪里去了?

那荣耀和梦境,现在哪里去了?

5

我们的出生,只是沉睡和遗忘:

共我们升起的灵,生命的大星,

本已坠往另一个地方,

又自远处莅临;

不是完全的失忆,

又非绝对的白纸,

曳着荣耀之云,我们是

从上帝那边来的孩子:

天堂迤逦在我们的幼年!

而那监牢的阴影会慢慢

把少年人围拢,

但他看到那光,和它的源泉,

他见了就兴意冲冲;

青年人渐离了东方,

他必得漫游,尚能将自然颂扬。

他的旅途依然

为瑰丽的想象所陪伴。

最终,这灵光黯淡于成年人的视野,

并在寻常的日光中消灭。

6

大地满载着属于她的愉悦;

也自有其天性里诸多的渴望,

甚至某种母性的柔肠,

以及并非无谓的目标,

这家常的保姆尽其所能

要令她哺育的孩子——和她同住的人,

忘却那诞生他的华美宫阙,

以及他熟知的荣耀。

7

瞧这个孩子,置身于初生的狂喜,
可爱的六岁幼童!
看,他躺在亲手做出的物件中,
烦躁于母亲迸放的吻,
又为父亲的目光所凝视!
看,在他脚边,一些小小的图样,
人生憧憬的斑斓碎片,
他新学的技艺赋予其形状;
婚礼抑或庆典,
葬礼抑或悼念;
——涌入他的心灵,
——化作他的歌唱:
此后他将让舌头屈从于
有关事务、爱情乃至斗争的谈论
然而无需太久,
这些又将被抛却,
伴随新的骄傲与欢悦
这小小的演员默记起另一段台词;
他的"谐剧舞台"上轮流充斥着
生活马车载乘的所有角色,
直至衰朽的岁月;

仿佛其一生的天命

不过是无尽的模仿。

8
你，外在的形体并不能相称
你灵魂的浩瀚；
你最好的哲人，仍固守着
遗产，你盲人中的慧眼，
不听不语，却洞彻
为不朽心灵所追求的永恒之渊，——
伟大的智者！有福的先知！
你掌握的真理，
我们曾毕生探寻，
却仍迷失在黑暗中，那墓穴的黑暗；
你的永生，犹如主之于奴，
凌驾于你的形体之上，白日一般，
一种不可弃掷的存在；
你这孩童，在你生命的高处
散播天生自由的光辉热力，
为何要付出这般热切的痛楚，
来惹岁月带来不可挣脱的桎梏，
这样与自己的幸福茫昧地抗争？

很快，你的灵将吸入尘世的重，
有分量的习俗也会压迫你的心胸，
沉似冰霜，深如生命。

9
多好啊！我们的余烬
尚残存一丝活力，
大自然还能唤醒
那些太容易消失的记忆！
我一想起我们的过去，就会生起
无尽的感激：这不是
为那些最值得赐福之物；
欢乐和自由，童年单纯的教义，
无论欢闹还是静默，
他的心里总扑腾着希望的翅羽。
我不是为了这些
才唱出感谢和赞美的歌；
而是为那些对感官和外在世界
所作的倔强究诘，
为那些来自我们身上的跌落，和湮灭；
为一个生灵茫然的惧怕
他正游荡在这不真实的凡尘，

为强烈的本能，面对它
我们的人性颤栗如丑事败露的罪人：
是为那些最初的情意，
那些模糊的往事，
如何称谓暂且不管，
那是我们一生的光源，
是我们眼中最明亮的灯；
支撑我们，疼爱我们，并有能力
使我们的喧嚣流年如同
永恒寂静中的瞬间：真理苏醒了
就不会毁灭：
任凭倦怠抑或暴烈，
也不论长幼，
所有与欢乐为敌的，都无法
完全将之消灭或摧垮！
因此在平静无风的季节里，
尽管我们远在内陆之上，
我们的灵仍看得见不朽的海洋，
它把我们送到了这里，
我们在瞬间依旧能重返那里，
去看那海岸上孩童的奔跑，
去听那奔腾不息的浩浩浪涛。

10

然后唱吧,你们这些鸟儿,唱,唱一曲欢乐的歌!

催促年轻的羊羔跳蹦

像踏着鼓声的叮咚!

我们在心里加入你们的阵营,

你们尖叫你们嬉戏,

五月的欢愉如今已

渗入你们的心里!

尽管那曾经的灿烂光辉

已永远从我眼中消退,

尽管没有什么能够重现

鲜花和青草中的荣耀流年;

我们并不为此悲伤,而是继续探寻

某种活力,在残存的往昔中;

在那原初的、一旦萌生

就不会泯灭的同情心中;

在那些源于人类苦难的

精神慰藉中;

在窥破死生的信念中,

在那些孕育哲思的岁月中。

11

哦，泉水，草地，山川，果园，
我们之间的爱恋永不会断！
我心深处感受到你们的伟力；
我只是舍弃了某一种乐事
却活在你们更为内在的支配下。
我爱那沿路奔流的小溪，
甚过当初我如它们一般轻快的时节；
每一个新生的日子依旧有
纯洁可爱的曙光；
那聚集在落日周围的云彩
在一双审视过人类必死性的眼睛里
正散发着庄重严肃的色泽；
又一段赛程结束，又一场新的胜利。
感谢我们赖以生存的人类心灵，
感谢它的温柔、欢乐与忧惧
对于我，最卑微的野花也能唤起
那泪水不及的最深处的思绪。

图书在版编目（CIP）数据

悼念集：汉英双语 / (英) 丁尼生著；张定浩译. -- 上海：上海文艺出版社, 2021
(2023.1重印)
(艺文志. 诗)
ISBN 978-7-5321-6922-1

Ⅰ.①悼… Ⅱ.①丁… ②张… Ⅲ.①诗集－英国－现代－汉、英 Ⅳ.①I561.25

中国版本图书馆CIP数据核字(2020)第270575号

发 行 人：毕　胜
策划编辑：肖海鸥
责任编辑：余静双
封面设计：张　卉 / halo-pages.com
内文制作：常　亭

书　　名：悼念集：汉英双语
作　　者：(英)丁尼生
译　　者：张定浩
出　　版：上海世纪出版集团　　上海文艺出版社
地　　址：上海市闵行区号景路159弄A座2楼　201101
发　　行：上海文艺出版社发行中心
　　　　　上海市闵行区号景路159弄A座2楼206室　201101　www.ewen.co
印　　刷：苏州市越洋印刷有限公司
开　　本：1092×787　1/32
印　　张：15
插　　页：4
字　　数：86,000
印　　次：2021年10月第1版　2023年1月第2次印刷
I S B N：978-7-5321-6922-1/I.6254
定　　价：68.00元
告　读　者：如发现本书有质量问题请与印刷厂质量科联系　T：0512-68180628